LIVING SPRINGS PUBLISHERS
PRESENTS:

STORIES THROUGH THE AGES
COLLEGE EDITION
2018

Compiled and edited by:

Dan Peavler, Henry E. Peavler and Jacqueline Veryle Peavler

Introduction by: Dan Peavler and Henry E. Peavler

**Living Springs
Publishers**

Each story in this collection is a work created from the imagination or experience of the author. The views expressed in the stories do not necessarily reflect the views of Living Spring Publishers L.L.P.

Living Springs Publishers
www.LivingSpringsPublishers.com

Cover design by Jacqueline Veryle Peavler

Cover Image:
Copyright: <a href='https://www.123rf.com/profile_sakkmesterke'>sakkmesterke / 123RF Stock Photo</a>

This book is dedicated to the authors who are
willing to take a chance and have their story judged.

Success is always to be found on the other side of
fear ~Unknown

Contents

Synopses

VAMPIRES KISS: Dorian T. Chase provides a new twist on an old story. Every night, the monsters come out to feed on the unsuspecting public. For a certain vampire, this night started out no different than any other. Then he sees her, the beautiful Veronica, and falls in love at first sight. As his animalistic desires fight between turning her, killing her, or letting her go, he comes to realize he's not the only monster out that night. Soon, he must choose Veronica's fate and decide whether he will take the plunge and deliver her a vampire's kiss. Dorian attends Wright State University.

A SMALL TOWN: Kelly Doyle has created a powerful story of the dynamics of a small community. A terrible crime is committed--the line between right and wrong is blurred. The readers are left to wonder who was the victim and who was the perpetrator. Kelly is a student at Emory University

LAWS OF THE LIVING HOUSE: Amanda Hemphill creates a vivid anthropomorphic portrayal of a house that isn't controlled by its owner. In fact, the owner is a long term prisoner, or more accurately, a caretaker for the fiendish needs of the place. She eventually finds that her time for providing for those desires is over in a ghastly sort of way. Amanda attends Eastern Shore Community College.

THE COTTAGE BY THE RIVER: Teresa Juarez creates a beautiful and sometimes humorous love story between a young couple, Cali and Andy, and their unborn child. As with many love stories this one ends tragically only to be reborn in a different form—the characters are real and their love, despite the tragedies, will last forever. Teresa is a student at the University of Colorado at Denver.

ORDER OF THE SPACE ZOMBIES: Mary Marley Latham has created a character who is determined to become a space zombie, an exclusive group that requires formal acceptance. The resulting application cover letter is both hilarious and poignant. Mary attends Southern Illinois University of Carbondale.

ONE MILLION NAMES FOR CINDERELLA: Nina Moldawsky gives us a marvelous story about a young woman who is forced by unforeseen circumstances to visit an aunt in London. There she meets Ali, an obnoxious know-it-all who really does know it all, until she finds the one thing he doesn't. Nina is a student at Columbia College in Chicago.

ON FRONT LAWNS: Isabelle Mongeau has written an absolutely fantastic story of childhood emotions seen from the viewpoint of a little girl who lives a seemingly normal life. With a dysfunctional mother and a new, mysterious neighbor the story is intense and thought provoking on many levels. This is a must read. Isabelle is a student at Emory University.

PRECOGNITION: Emily Porter introduces us to a man who is blessed, actually as it turns out cursed, with having his nightly dreams come true. He tries valiantly to control this unwanted gift and succeeds, until one mistake leads to disaster. This story is delightful and entertaining throughout. Emily attends Hofstra University.

PEELED BACK AND LIFTED: JQ Salazar shares a delightfully real story of a young man, Dom, who is faced with the death of a relative. He tries to clarify what Uncle Morris meant to him, how he fit into the family relationship. In the process Dom discovers a little more about himself. This is wonderful reading, both meaningful and entertaining. JQ is a student at the University of Colorado at Denver.

FROM THE WINDOW OF A HEART HOSPITAL IN CLOVIS: Sierra Saykeo has delivered a poignant portrayal of the responsibilities and emotions involved with caring for an aging parent. Heartfelt and sensitive, this story carries us through a gamut of feelings including humor and despair. It is a must read for everyone. Sierra is a student at Guilford College.

DEATH COMES FOR ALL THINGS: Fiona Shampine has written a fantasy born from the same stock as the ancient Greek Gods of mythology. She delves into the realm of those mighty and powerful figures only to find that their emotions are very human-like after all. The reader is enthralled all the way through the surprise ending. Fiona attends Columbia College in Chicago.

FIRE AND ICE: Nia Tipton gives us an unconventional love story that is tinged with the prejudices of many cultures, on many different levels. It is touching and thought provoking, and can create controversy, but in the end it is the love story of a young man from birth to young adulthood. Excellent reading! Nia is a student at Columbia College in Chicago.

LIFE IN COLOR: Sarah Vita presents a story that is probably as old as time--dreams of unexpected wealth and what can be done with it. Gavin Hayes is an average man who loses a good job at the bank only to discover a treasure in a very unlikely place. The beauty of this story is how Gavin manages his new found prosperity. Beautifully crafted and believable! Sarah is a student at Merrimack College.

CRITICAL NONCONFORMITY: What would the world be like if every living person looked, acted, and thought exactly the same? In the world Connor J. Walcott has created, this frightening possibility has become a reality. Well written and plausible, this story shows the effect of genetic engineering and government control gone horribly wrong, and follows one man's search for individuality in an identical society. Connor attends Florida Atlantic University.

THE MUSIC BOX OF SOULS: Cassandra Winnie has given us a story of a dancer who receives a break when the lead in a ballet disappears and she is called to fill the position. In an Edgar Allen Poe twist, she becomes the star in a story that she could not have foreseen. If you enjoy dark mysteries this story is for you. Cassandra attends Caldwell University.

DEEP PURPLE: Jamie Sharon Wright has written a wonderful story of a child and her relationship with her mothers. The emotions are well defined and realistic, almost as if we are there experiencing this tragedy ourselves. It is a wonderfully crafted story! Jamie attends Colorado State University

Introduction

Cultural manifestations often define the content and tone used by storytellers. But many of the stories Living Springs Publishers chose for our second annual Stories Through the Ages 2018 book have themes that are throwback to decades gone by, which makes for a great contrast with other stories of reality.

Readers will enjoy stories ranging from vampires and haunted houses, to stories about life in a small town and a cottage by the river, all wonderfully entertaining and well written. The submissions we received are unique, diverse, and captivating giving every reader something to look forward to. We want to congratulate the sixteen talented authors who are featured in this year's book.

Many of the submissions we received that did not make it into the book were very good. All entries were evaluated without the judge's knowledge of who wrote it or where the manuscript originated. Surprisingly, even though we received stories from many different colleges across the county the 2018 winner is from Emory University in Atlanta, Georgia, the same university last year's winner attends.

This congregating of successful writers is nothing new. In Paris, France, in the 1920's you might have encountered Earnest Hemingway, T.S. Elliot, Gertrude Stein, F. Scott Fitzgerald, Ford Mattox Ford, James Joyce and others. Creative writing is a taxing and solitary endeavor that requires feedback, determination and a thick skin. Allowing your creation to be read by others is daunting and those of us who choose to scribble down our innermost thoughts and put them on public display enjoy the company of those not afraid to do the same.

It is important to Living Spring Publishers to give writers the freedom to write about whatever it is that inspires them. We hope that all authors who submitted stories understand that writing is about broadening your existence, creating your own world through your own ideas and imagination.

Story telling is a terrific way to communicate one's ideas. Leaving an impression in a total stranger's mind is a powerful gift. Because everyone has a story to tell, Living Springs Publishers is pleased to give so many talented authors an avenue to have their work published. Someone once stated, "those at the top of a mountain didn't fall there." We understand the effort, fortitude, and hard work it takes to create a story. For this we thank all the authors who had the courage to submit their work. It has allowed us to publish a wonderful and entertaining book.

On Front Lawns
By Isabelle Mongeau

I sat on the windowsill, hands and forehead pressed against the glass, watching the new neighbors. It was the first time in my twelve years on this street that someone was moving in, and not out. Never mind a family that had just a girl, an older woman, and a three-legged dog. The red-headed girl looked my age, her bony arms gripping a box too big for her, her stick legs treading up the uneven cement steps to their one story white house with green shutters. The strong-boned, pepper-haired woman tugged a suitcase across the lawn and the Golden Retriever jumped up and down, wagging her tail.

"They got a dog with only one front leg," I said and my breath fogged up the surface. "It's got a bandage and everything."

I heard a swish of liquid. I didn't need to look to know she had sprawled herself out on the couch, again. The TV flashed at her.

"Why don't you go say hi? Mama needs to rest."

She always needed to rest. I climbed down from my perch and ignored her request for a kiss on the cheek. I left the family room and the screen door banged behind me like cymbals clashing. I walked barefoot to the edge of our soggy, brown grass, when the girl came out the front door, the dog circling around her. She spotted me.

"Whatcha looking at?"

"Your dog is funny looking." I tugged at my tangled hair, eyeing the bounce and curl in hers. She crossed her arms.

"Her name is Ginger." The dog leaned her bandaged side against the girl's thigh. "And you don't got shoes on, that's funny looking."

"Well, Ginger's only got three legs." I curled my toes and cool water squished between them. She stepped into the muddy street. Ginger followed.

"So? You only got two."

"Suppose you're right." She didn't wilt away like the other kids did when I talked to them. I took a step forward, the cool gravely pavement pressed up against the bottoms of my feet. She came closer and stuck out a pale hand.

"I'm Livia. My name comes from this powerful woman who was married to Caesar."

"Like Caesar salad?" No one ever shook my hand, especially not kids. I took hers.

She stuck her hands back on her bony hips, elbows poking out in the air like twigs snapped in half.

"I think so. What are you named after?"

My cheeks warmed in the cold air. People like me weren't named after anything.

"I'm Chloe." I glanced down. "It means barefoot."

Their front door opened and the older woman stepped out.

"Oh, hello there."

"Nana, this is Chloe," Livia said.

"How is it May? It feels like March." Her grandmother approached us, rubbing her arm. She was tall and broad, not like those small, shriveled old people, but still had an oval face like crinkled paper. Her sharp, black eyes scraped over me like a peeler over a potato. She shook my hand, too. "I'm Mrs. Jameson. It's a little chilly for no shoes, don't you think?"

I wasn't sure what May felt like where they came from, but for us it was one of those dribble months, when the snow seeps into the Earth and doesn't dry up fully until July. When the cracked pavement bleeds with dark, thick mud and people trek in rain boots to the main street for groceries. To me, dirt felt just as good under my feet as mud, which felt just as good as grass. Wet or dry.

"I'll wear no shoes any time," I said.

"Nana, I'm gonna stop wearing shoes, too."

"Out of the question." Mrs. Jameson looked at me. "Is your mother or father home? I'd love to meet them."

"Daddy's gone and Mama's at work right now." I chewed the inside of my cheek.

"Maybe when she comes home, then."

"She works a lot."

Mrs. Jameson nodded. "Alright, well I have to finish unpacking. Nice to meet you."

We watched her grandmother walk towards the white moving van. When she was out of earshot, I turned back to Livia.

"Are you coming to our school now?"

She shook her head.

"Why not?"

"Because I'm too smart. I'm named after Livia, remember?"

"That's stupid." A cool wind blew across us and goose bumps dimpled my arms. I brushed the hair out of my eyes, wincing at a tender spot near my temple.

"I think you're stupid for going." Livia grinned and her eyes watched my hand. "But I like your hair."

***

The next morning, I got ready for school and walked to the edge of my lawn to wait for Livia. She never came out so I walked to school alone. She didn't come to class, either. I asked my teacher who Caesar and Livia were. She said Caesar was the greatest emperor of the greatest empire, a long time ago. I said doesn't seem like it because I never heard of him before. She said only adults know Augustus Caesar. I asked her why his first name was a month. She sent me away.

When the day finished and all the kids poured out to their streets like beer from a bottle, Livia was playing on the front lawn, throwing a tennis ball to Ginger. She spotted me padding down the street towards our houses and waved, forming a neon green arch in the air.

"Wanna play?"

Sweat prickled my body. *She* wanted to play with *me?* The note crumpled in my hand, awaiting Mama's signature, said I wasn't allowed to play with the Quinn boy at recess anymore. I wiped a clammy palm on my thigh.

"First, I have to write Mama's name on this. It's gotta look different from how I write."

"I can write her name."

I retrieved a pen from my bag. She pressed the paper onto my back and wrote as I spelled out Mama's name. I felt the pressure of each letter: H-A-R-P-E-R.

"I have some extra sneakers if you want them. They don't have holes in them like yours." Before I could say anything, she pulled the paper away from my back and handed me the note. "What did Quinn do?"

I bit my lip, and thought about how the glowing arch would be replaced with a sharp stare once I told her.

"I punched him because he tried to kiss my cheek," I finally said.

"Boys are gross." Her eyes widened and she giggled. I grinned myself.

"I broke his nose."

She laughed and gave me a high five.

***

The last month of school flew by, instead of dribbling on like it usually does. Each morning, I paused at the verge of my brown grass, waiting, before walking to school alone. In the afternoons, Livia and I would take off our shoes (but only when Mrs. Jameson was too busy to notice) and lie on our backs in the grass, competing about who can tell the better story from the shapes in the clouds.

When the afternoons were done, I'd check the mailbox for a letter from my uncle. He usually sent us a white envelope each month, and the next day, Mama would buy bags full of bananas and chocolate and gin. I would eat until I couldn't remember what that constant gnawing felt like the rest of the month and Mama would drink until she couldn't remember at all. The past couple months, the mailbox had remained empty. Sometimes, the home phone would ring and Mama would pick it up to scream and hang up.

I checked the mailbox on my walk home from the last day of school. Nothing. So May had completely galloped along with no mail, except pink bills, and no Livia at school.

The tennis ball bumped into my heel. I shot a look over my shoulder to see Livia crossing the street. Ginger lurched past her and towards the ball. She no longer wore the bandage, and when she jumped around me, her stump brushed my thigh. I hated it but patted her side, anyway.

"Hey, why didn't you go to school, ever?"

"Nana said I needed some time off to...to feel better." She shrugged.

"About what—"

A shriek stabbed the air and Livia grabbed my arm.

"What was that?"

The scream pierced again. I shook her off and sprinted straight for my screen door. It clanked against its frame as I stopped short in the dim house.

Mama leaned against the countertop, like a weak tree slanting to one side when its trunk was rotted and full of bugs. She rested her head in one hand, while the other held a piece of paper, shaking like leaves in a storm. An empty beer bottle sat next to her. She didn't look up.

"I'm waiting on a final payment your uncle was supposed to give me by now. It was supposed to be a lot of money but I didn't get it last month. At first I thought, that's all right, it always takes lawyers some time with these things. But now those government bastards turned off our lights."

"I'm sorry, Mama." I swallowed. I always said this when I didn't know what else to do to help her.

"It isn't your fault, baby."

"Why don't you get your job back?" I set my backpack down by the door.

"You know I can't. I hate talking to customers and the manager doesn't like me."

I blew air out of my nostrils and took off my sneakers because if I had something to do, I didn't have anything to say.

I've only seen my uncle once, after Daddy left. He had the car running in the driveway with his family inside. He told Mama that he loved her and she said love didn't exist for people like them. Maybe if he had stayed longer, he could've helped. I peeled the socks off, and walked closer to her.

"When was the last time you went to the restaurant?" I asked.

"I fucking can't. Your uncle should really send money—"

"If we had our own money, then—"

"Shut up, Chloe."

"—we wouldn't need his, then. Ever think about that?"

"Shut up!" She screamed and slammed the beer bottle on the floor next to me. The glass exploded like a firecracker, shards stinging my left leg. The anger dissipated to fear and slithered back down into my stomach to hide. I didn't break her gaze when warm blood dribbled down to the tiles. She grabbed my face, yanking me to her, my feet scraping against the glass. I bit my lip as tears welled up in my eyes. I could see the veins in her eyes, like red spider webs.

"You don't know what it was like in my house. I took the blows for my brother. I always got between him and our daddy when he drank. Wanna see my back? Do you?"

Droplets of her spit sprinkled my face. I didn't move. I didn't reply whenever she talked about the scars she had. Daddy said she was haunted and sometimes the ghosts took over her. I didn't blame him for going.

"You know why I took those hits for my brother? Because my mama just watched and let it happen." Tears spilled down her face. "She was supposed to protect us, that's what a mother does. But she didn't. *That's* why your uncle should send his big sister money. You got that?"

I nodded.

"I would never let anyone hurt you like that. You know that."

"What's going on?"

I yanked myself from Mama's grip and whipped around. Livia stood in the doorway, Ginger behind her. Embarrassment squeezed around my heart until I thought it would pop. I stepped in front of the glass.

"Who's that?" Mama asked, her voice faint now. Her ghosts always sucked up her energy. No one said anything. I heard her sigh before sauntering to the couch. My eyes followed her until turning onto my friend.

"Get out, Livia."

"Why?"

"Leave!"

"But what happened—"

I rushed forward, ignoring the slick blood beneath my feet, and shoved her out of the doorway. She latched onto my forearm, pulling me with her. We stumbled down the front steps and tripped over Ginger, who yelped and scampered out of the way. Livia jerked back, eyes watching me, her body panting.

"You're bleeding."

"You're snooping," I said over Ginger's barks. I turned to her. "Shut up!"

Livia's brows furrowed. "She didn't do anything to you."

I clenched and unclenched my fists. "She's got three legs. She's useless and stupid."

"You're stupid for fighting with your mom."

"You don't know what you're talking about." I spat on the grass.

Livia crossed her arms. "Oh yeah? What did you do this time? Punch her in the nose because she tried to kiss your cheek?"

I lunged and tackled her into the patchy grass, me on top of her.

"You bastard!" A pain kept stabbing over and over in my chest. "You stupid idiot!"

I hit her face but the pain just grew. I punched again and again, tears gushing from my eyes, my knuckles warm with blood. Ginger barked. Livia screamed and slapped me, my face snapping to the side. I stopped.

She grabbed my shoulders and shoved me off her. She sat on my stomach. Tears cut through a red rose that blossomed in the center of her face. She spat a mouthful of blood on my forehead.

"Listen, dummy. I would give anything to be able to fight with my mom and daddy again."

"Haven't seen my daddy in five years because Mama is crazy." I pushed her off me and we sat staring at each other, pieces of shriveled grass caught in our hair.

"It's better to have crazy parents than no parents," Livia said.

"I gotta live with her. You can picture yours how you want."

"I picture them dead, because that's what they are."

My gaze dropped to my stained hands. There were curls of red hair stuck to my palms. I wiped them on the grass. We sat in silence until the sun drifted low in the sky. Nothing seemed right.

When I got back inside the house, with the blood dried on my feet and legs and the bruise on my face, the glass still lay scattered about the floor. Now that the sun was leaving, the room darkened. She lay on the couch. When the door banged shut, she drew herself up.

"Hi, baby."

"Hi, Mama."

She got up from the couch, swept across the carpet to the tiles, and stepped over the glass. She opened the fridge and its white light spilled out. She bumped the door closed with her hip and keyed open a beer.

"Do you love me?"

"Yes, Mama."

"Am I good mother?" Her eyes bore into mine.

"Yes, Mama."

***

Later, she laid on the couch. I sat in front of her. We watched the black TV.

"It'll come back on," she said in the dark and silence.

"How?" I whispered.

She made another drink and said nothing. So, I said nothing. When her breathing slowed and the glasses were empty, I tugged on her arm to get her into bed. She refused. I left her on the couch and cleaned up the glass, sweeping the shards into the dustpan and dropping them into the trash. I grabbed a matchbox from the pantry and headed to the bathroom.

The bathroom was like a little box that time forgot, and a place I just wanted to crawl into. From the candles around the sink that Mama used to light for their smell, to the makeup behind the mirror she used to wear. I lit the wicks, the flame burning my thumb, and saw the flicker of my plain reflection.

I looked at my legs, the skin appearing even paler with the splotches of red smudged across it. I peeled off my clothes and climbed into the tub. When I trickled cool water on my legs, the crackled patches melted away, swirling down the drain in rivers of pink. I picked out chips of glass from my skin, the beads tapping against the tub's surface. All that was left were deep lines.

I laid down and felt the crisp water spread across my back. Mama's words rang in my ear. *Wanna know what happens when you try to protect someone you love?*

My other hand traced the pattern of scars on my side, just below my ribs.

I already know, Mama.

Mrs. Jameson rapped on our door at 1pm the next day. Mama was deep in sleep, strung out on the couch. I saw the large, strong-boned, square woman, with one hand clutching a leash that held Ginger through the screen. She smiled when she saw me.

"How are you?" She asked.

"I'm fine, you?"

"Why don't you get your sneakers on and come join us for a walk?"

The sky was a dull grey, the air was muggy. Ginger trotted ahead of us with the leash taunt, drops of slobber sprinkling the pavement from her pink tongue. I eyed Mrs. Jameson in the silence, my T-shirt itchy and hot with my sweat. We walked halfway around the block before she said anything.

"I saw Livia's face."

I watched my legs and said nothing. I heard her sigh.

"She told me about the fight and what you said to each other."

Again, I kept my face hidden from her, my lips squeezed tight. What I usually do when Mama gets mad and I just want it to pass.

"Did Livia tell you why Ginger only has three legs?" She asks.

I shook my head. We looped around the block and approached our street again.

"She was in the car with Livia's parents," she said. "The only thing that survived the crash was Ginger and three of her legs."

I stopped in the middle of the street, right between our two houses. Livia's words rang in my ear, *Nana said I needed some time off to feel better.*

"Chloe!"

I yanked away from Mrs. Jameson and brushed hair out of my eyes. Mama stood in the doorway, pressing against the frame with a knife in her hand. She watched me.

"I'm making breakfast. Why don't you come inside?"

"Go with your mama." Mrs. Jameson stiffened next to me and turned away.

But my mama was already coming to us, her bare feet stepping into the squishy grass, the blade in her hand looking as dull as the sky.

"What's going on…."

She stopped and her face drained of any grey color.

"You."

"What?" I said.

Her eyes glued to Mrs. Jameson, who faced her, letting go of Ginger's leash. The dog padded towards their lawn and scratched at the door. Mama stuck her free hand on her hip, elbow protruding out like a branch snapped in half.

"What are you doing here?"

"This is Livia's…"

I watched the two of them, their similarities unfolding in front of my eyes. The way they stood with their Amazonian frames, the way they talked, the way they acted. *Love doesn't exist for people like us,* Mama had said back when my uncle came. Back when he left the car running in the driveway. Back when I sat at the window and saw the red-haired woman sitting in the front seat, a redheaded child in the back.

No money came from my uncle in months, the uncle in the car when it crashed. Mama said one last, final payment, *it always takes lawyers some time with these things.* A will.

"Hi baby," Mrs. Jameson said.

"Don't you fucking call me that." Mama rewrapped her fingers around the knife.

"I missed you. I wished you came to your brother's funeral—"

"Shut up! What do you think you're doing talking to my daughter?"

"I want to be there for her." Mrs. Jameson blinked. Mama spat at Mrs. Jameson's feet.

"You don't deserve to. Baby, come here."

"She's nice to me." I wiped the droplets away. Mama craned her neck, her eyes narrowing.

"Well, she wasn't nice to me, how 'bout that."

Livia opened the door and noticed the three of us. Sweat dribbled down my face but I didn't move. She walked across the street, Ginger at her side.

"Is everything okay?"

"Stay over there, Livia." I watched the knife, my chest frozen. Mrs. Jameson tugged on her hair.

"These girls are my last chance. I need to…they're my shot at being—"

"What about your own child, huh?" Mama pointed the knife at her.

"Mama, you need to calm down."

The knife waved towards me, a foot from my face. "Don't tell me to calm down. If this woman is so nice to you, wanna see my back? Huh? Wanna see the scars?"

The world seemed to collapse into itself, and it was just Mama and me. I heard Livia say something but it was like speaking through thick glass. My fists clamped shut, then spread out flat, then clenched again. I looked at Mama, the tip of her knife pointed at my nose.

"Show me."

At first, she just stared at me. Then, she threw her head back in laughter.

"You couldn't handle it."

In the past, I've turned my gaze away. Not this time.

"I dare you."

Mama's eyes sharpened.

She pulled the neckline of her shirt from her body and ran the knife down its middle. The cheap cloth ripped open like a jacket and she snapped the rest off. She turned around, and the red spider webs in her eyes were displayed in nude across her back. Lines of ridges and valleys cut in patterns between her shoulder blades and trailing her spine. Cigarette burns fell in a waterfall down her upper arm.

She faced me again, panting, gripping the knife. Her bare breasts hung low as her shoulders hunched forward. Her eyes locked on Mrs. Jameson.

"This is what you let happen."

Rage exploded in my chest. I pulled my own shirt over my head to show the nude spider web that spread across my stomach.

"And this is what you did."

Mama winced.

"Do you even remember?" I asked. "Or were you too drunk?"

Did she know about the times she locked me in the closet? The times she smashed her bottles on me? The times the wedding ring caught and tore the flesh? Had she ever comprehended that I knew she was going to hurt someone and I didn't want it to be herself?

Oh, some part of her must've been conscious for all of it, even if it wasn't her heart. She knew. She just chose to forget and I chose to blame it on her ghosts.

Livia began to cry. I balled my fists.

"Go away, Livia."

"No." She shook her head. "I want to be here. I'm your friend, Chloe."

I blinked. Something inside me unlocked, softened.

Mama stared at me. The knife slipped out of her hand and she collapsed onto her knees in the brown lawn, shoulders shaking. Her wails wafted into the air like smoke.

"I'm so sorry."

I didn't move. No one did. I itched for the knife so close to me now. Mama grappled for my hand and her face streamed with tears and snot.

"Do you love me? I know I've made mistakes, but do you love me?"

"Yes, Mama."

"Am I a good mother?"

My eyes flicked towards the knife, then up at Livia and her bruised face. I thought about the blood and red hair on my hands. She clutched onto our grandmother. Mrs. Jameson watched, her oval face stripped with regret and sadness. Mama's eyes swam.

"Baby? Am I?"

I kicked the knife away from us with my new sneaker.

"No, Harper, you're not."

Isabelle Mongeau

Isabelle Mongeau studies Creative Writing and Film at Emory University in Georgia. Though she loves life in Atlanta, she was raised in Wellesley, Massachusetts. From an early age, Isabelle learned

that the fastest way to travel was to pick up a book. Besides opening up new worlds to her, she attributes much of her empathy and compassion to reading, and believes all children should have the experience of enjoying a good book. In addition to Living Springs Publishers, Isabelle has been published in Emory's literary magazine, *Alloy*. Isabelle seeks to create stories that are both serious and entertaining. She is never short on inspiration as she is one of four children (excluding the family's two giant, fluffy dogs, Ginger and Jake as "children", though her mom may disagree). Isabelle comes from reading parents, and her mother, Kelley, is her first reader. She would like to thank her family and friends for their endless support.

Peeled Back, and Lifted
By JQ Salazar

Uncle Morris died yesterday. It was my day off.

Eva was pulling a double shift at the hospital and I got stuck cleaning, doing laundry, dishes. You know, the works. I had just sat down to surf the web when I got the call from my dad.

"Remember your Uncle Morris?" His chilly voice crawled into my ear.

I hadn't seen Morris in five years. Last summer, word traveled that he'd gotten lung cancer. He slipped into a coma and I'm pretty sure everyone assumed the worst, so when he woke up a few days later there was, at least for me, a stunted surprise. Then I forgot.

"Well you know what they say, dead as a dodo." From someone else this would have been shocking, but Dad always had a way of burying his anguish in punchlines. They were never funny.

"I had a feeling. So. What happens now?" My mind was already jumping ahead to plane flights and spending money I didn't have; to breaking up the routine of my comfortable, boring life. It's when these things happen that you realize the cost you're paying to be *away*. My whole family lived within a few hours of each other in

Florida but I was the only one on the west coast. The cost to alienate oneself.

"That's the thing, Dom. There's not gonna be a funeral. Or a wake."

"What?" I sat up in my chair.

"I'm not really sure, to be honest. I'm getting all the information secondhand through my brothers. You know how it was with me and Morris." He coughed nervously.

I only knew in the vaguest of senses 'how it was' between them. I hadn't seen much of my dad's side of the family since I was in high school, and even then I understood that there was some kind of awkward social boundary between them all. Like physics distorted when they got together, and there were rough, jagged lines of electricity jutting everywhere. Some of the family were televisions and some were magnets; so being in the same room together, even once a year for a holiday, was implosive. I was always too young, and now I was too far away. Soon I'd be too hollow, the memories too dim.

"Yeah, I guess." I spared myself the usual *there's a lot you don't understand* speech that Dad tended to hand out. "How old was he?"

"73. Hell, that's gonna be me in a few years!" He forced a laugh and a moment of silence passed between us. "I'll call you if anything changes. I just wanted to make sure you knew. Dead as a doornail."

I hung up and just sort of sat there, trying to think of memories, searching the Uncle Morris category of my brain. It wasn't easy since I mostly remembered him from when I was 11 or 12. Just passing glances, a memorable laugh or two. How he stood in a button-up shirt and battered slacks, maybe lighting a fresh cigarette, stuffing the lighter in his pocket. He looked like Robert Mitchum, hair slicked back, silhouetted in a doorway. He always had this strange energy, like he'd cracked the secret to gravity and was living on a plain that was twenty percent lighter than ours.

I remembered answering the phone when he called for my dad one time.

"Hello?" My squeaky voice cracked.

There was silence for a second, until I heard Uncle Morris lean in to deliver a throaty, "Hey." It sounded like the start of a joke, "Is this. D*om*?" Like he knew something about you that you didn't. Like he was too cool.

———

I could only find two pictures of him. Both of them nearly identical; he was sitting in the distance, half-smiling at an impromptu photo. Both of them were exactly how I'd pictured him anyway. Disappointing.

I needed something new, a fresh experience to tie this sudden news with. I had already stood and sat in the same handful of places in my apartment, already made monotonous memories out of menial tasks. I felt the need to commemorate Morris in some unique way, however indistinct it would actually be. So I sat on the kitchen floor, looked up at the window and watched the last pools of grey and blue sky drain into the distance. It was all pretty pathetic and I didn't feel sad. I wished I did.

Eva came home and got me talking. We ate and then laughed about the wackiness of families. She even got me to do an impersonation of Morris, which was complete dogshit and made me think of how she would never really be able to know what he was like. All she'd have were two photos and my Ed Wood-level impression. So I told her to just watch 'The Night of the Hunter' and consider that to be my uncle instead.

—

The next day, I caught the bus to work.

It was ugly outside. Rain poured into every crevice of the world. I watched the slums blur and smear beyond the bus windows. I was living in a painter's rendition of the city, a painter who had spilled water across the finished product and smudged out the details, wiping it all away.

I was physically present but my mind was an antenna, scanning the netherworlds for any ancient family recollections I might still have in me. I thought about how Uncle Morris wasn't technically my uncle, he was my dad's uncle. He was my grandmother's brother. I wasn't even sure what to really call him, a great uncle? He was as far removed from me as my memories were of him.

I tried to remember times where Morris was around but couldn't actually recall anything specific. He was always a bit of a phantom on the fringes of family gatherings, one that floated in and hung out in the background of what I could remember. If everyone was at the dinner table, he was sitting at the counter. If everyone was opening Christmas presents, he was outside having a smoke. He was elusive.

———

I thought of the last time I saw him. I was on my way to the west coast. He happened to be along my route.

Leaves were blowing everywhere as I pulled into the driveway. I was 23 and he stared me down with his killer grin. He was more weathered and beaten down than I'd remembered, but still had the soul of Morris nonetheless.

"D*om*. How are ya, guy?"

"I'm good. Finally left the nest."

"Yeah?" As if he thought I might be lying. "How's mom? How's dad? How's the sister?" He sat in a chair, crossed his legs and lit up a smoke. He leaned back; a detective waiting for his suspect to spill their guts. The man belonged in noirs and spaghetti westerns.

I couldn't remember anything specific we talked about, but I was really taken aback by two things about the visit. The first was how the details of his house were just like the ones of my grandmother's house.

I spent a lot of time at Grandma's when I was very young, a place where everything was covered in cat hair or smelled like an ashtray. There were always mugs full of pens, staples or rubber bands lying around. Metal cookie boxes that became containers for old photos or drawings, brown paper grocery bags stacked up in a corner. So it was somewhat surprising to find that Uncle Morris had all that stuff too! I specifically recall a large rock that Grandma used as a doorstop for the patio, and whaddya know? Morris had one just like it. My relatives' interior lifestyles were made up from all these odd knickknacks, or what just about every little kid collectively called *weird old people stuff*.

I tapped my foot vigorously on the bus floor as I recognized this new perspective, this connection between Grandma and Uncle Morris's trinkets. It brought to mind tradition and habit, as well as individuality and a more humbled humanization of these two unknowable titans in my family tree.

I thought of their stubborn ticks and mannerisms, honing in on the absence of them in my own DNA. Who knew just how far back my bloodline had been hoarding cookie boxes and door-rocks? But more glaringly, why wasn't *I* in on these idiosyncrasies? Why hadn't I inherited these little quirks? It was as if Grandma and Morris had snipped the family tree behind themselves, robbing everyone down the line of some possible clan-like instincts. *You know how it was between me and Morris*. I felt annoyed, knowing that a tiny layer of the veil that was my family history had just been peeled back, and lifted.

—

The rain lightened to a mist, a cold fog blanketing the road in patches.

The bus came to a halt and the doors opened. On impulse I stood up and walked right into the street. I didn't know this part of town. I could smell the beach as I shuffled aimlessly into the grey horizon.

The second, and most important thing about my final Morris visit was the more identifiable one for me: How goddamn alone the man was.

His wife had died of cancer some 20 years before. On top of that, Morris's own middle-aged daughter died in a car accident not too long ago. And as far as I knew, he didn't have any other kids, and never remarried. At the time I only had a cloudy intuition of his situation, but on reexamination of the whole experience, all I could think was *what a life*. Here I was complaining about my lack of communication with the outer rim of my family, yet Uncle Morris had lost a lover and a child that were right in front of him. Events like that should've easily weighed him down with baggage, turning him into a magnet, toxic and destructive in his pull. But they didn't.

—

I passed through a deserted basketball court before finding the shoreline. The closer I got, the less dense the fog became and I realized there was a fire burning in a garbage can, buried right into the sand, maybe 15 feet from the water. I was confused, and couldn't see anyone around. The fire looked fresh, started no more than a minute or two before.

I sat down and watched the ocean stir lazily like a big puddle of slush. The fire was toasty but looked ridiculous; a small flamethrower in the middle of a smoky wasteland. Further down the shore I spotted a woman and child walking along the beach. The child seemed excited, jumping on all fours, picking up rocks and chucking them into the sea. The dull sunlight lit them up from behind, like dark vestiges imitating a mammal's movements. There was something unnatural about the light, which gave the whole thing a nightmarish quality.

As they approached, I found myself thinking of Morris's wife and daughter. Here they were, appearing as innocent shades on some abstract beach, representing what I imagined to be Morris's desire and ideal salvation, representing his twenty-plus years of solidarity and dread.

Or maybe they were speaking to me. Maybe these shadows were Eva and the child we hadn't made yet. Maybe it was a sign that they would die too, that I carried Morris's same dubious curse in my own blood. Or worse, maybe I was the dead one in the scenario and this was a life I'd leave behind.

Or maybe it was something else. The figures got much closer and I noticed that the woman was older, matured. Maybe it was Grandma and the child was me. Maybe this was that one time when I was four and we went to the beach in Naples. Where I cut my hand open while scooping up seashells. Where it was just Grandma and myself. They said we stayed three days but I only remembered three seconds.

I looked around but couldn't see the woman and child anymore.

I crafted a small mound of sand to rest my head on and checked my watch, bringing it to my ear to hear the ticking.

I remembered being seven years old, sitting at Grandma's dining table and messing with her metronome while she read the newspaper.

"Why's it so loud?"

She eyed me pensively before staring back at the paper, "It's only loud because you're being so quiet."

"Doesn't it bother you?"

"Only if you let it." She smiled to herself, "Besides, the cats don't mind."

Now, I understood the interaction on a deeper level. It was the smallest but most reassuring connection I could think of. A characteristic passed down. An acknowledgement that I belonged in my family's obscure and muted dynasty.

My watch ticked effortlessly. So in a minor triumph, I took a nap.

———

I woke up to a loud, sizzling sound; heavy rain dousing the fire. Sort of startled, I sat up in complete darkness, only able to see the city's lights down the shore. The rain had started back up, as lethal as it was abrupt.

As I trudged back through the sand towards the road, I thought of how silly I was, skipping work to sleep on the beach. I thought of Morris's playful laugh. Guttural and worn, but comforting even in the crappiest of times.

I was hit with a small epiphany: Uncle Morris had been there in the days before Grandma passed away.

———

I fell, back into the nursing home in south Florida, some 13 years ago. I was a senior in high school and Grandma was fading. The memories were hazy and mostly consisted of me leaning over her deathbed, surrounded by other family members. I moved through the moments and there, behind my parents, behind my cousins, I found a familiar face smirking at me.

Zoom in a little closer, enhance: *Uncle fucking Morris, you sly bastard, sneaking yourself into memories under the Grandma category.* I racked my head a bit more and was able to conjure up one specific scene. I replayed it in HD, relishing each nuanced beat.

We stood outside the nursing home as he smoked a cigarette.

"So. You see 'Casino Royale' yet?" His voice rose towards the end of the sentence, as if he was egging me on to do something bad.

"Uh, yeah. Best Bond ever."

He took a drag, "Yeah, yeah." Smoke blew out of his nostrils and he cocked his eyebrows, before smiling sharply, "But nothing tops 'From Russia With Love'". Then he laughed his infectious laugh.

His sister was on her way out and he hadn't let an ounce of sorrow slip. How did he do it? The man was a TV, holding in all the terror of life. He'd been warped and abused by the magnetic pull of his own ghosts but somehow managed not to shatter.

I probably had a good slew of Morris memories tucked up in there somewhere but they weren't just gonna tumble out at my request. I needed to let them all flow, to interweave and connect with each other, forming a blanket or a quilt that I could proudly fall into on my shittiest of days.

Maybe I didn't know the Morris that my dad knew. Maybe I never saw the darker side that others had. But that didn't change his comforting presence in the backdrop of my youth. It didn't change my empathy for his wherewithal. He was just a memorable somebody in my life, and I let that sink in.

———

Like some pointless joke, the rain let up once again as I approached my apartment building. When I opened the front door, the smell of a roast stopped me cold in my tracks.

My gorgeous Eva spun around from the kitchen with elegance, glowing like the personification of warmth and relaxation.

She stared at me hard and asked, "What the hell happened to you?"

I looked down at my clothes, soaked and covered in sand. I held out my arms to her and laughed inwardly.

I couldn't help but wonder whether I was a TV or a magnet.

JQ Salazar

JQ was born in Miami, Florida. He grew up on hip-hop and PlayStation 1 games. After high school, he completed a four-year stint in the US Air Force before moving to Denver, Colorado where he currently studies English at CU Denver. He considers himself to

be an optimistic realist, as well as a heavy reader, gamer and film enthusiast. You can find him navigating through Future Garage soundscapes and cyberpunk dreams. So, in other words, at home with his cat. This is his first publication.

Laws of the Living House
By Amanda Hemphill

Some things you're born knowing even before you understand them. Things that are written on the fabric of your DNA.

I was born with the Laws.

1. A living House brings the dead like a corpse brings flies. (Note: Two things that should not be just have a certain way of catching each other's attention.)

2. The living House can only be possessed by one owner at a time and must be passed on to the next generation or the house will die, and its owner with it.

3. The walls of a living House pulse in time to a heartbeat buried deep within. It stares at what the rest of the world ignores through deep-set eyes in sockets of dark corners; the dead fly to its quiet light like moths. (Note: The House will use this to its advantage.) (More-important-note: I'm accustomed to this. I'm so over it. Let it be known a few ghosts could never bother me.)

4. Any guest of the living House will be sacrificed to the House once their visit is complete in order to keep its owner youthful and healthy, thus more effective to protect the House.

5. The owner of the House cannot forfeit the house without passing it on to a new generation or dying with it. (Note: For the record, I had no intention of letting either of these things happening.)

"I don't know, I'm still not totally sold on the color. Too much like mustard. What says you, Red?"

The paintbrush glides across the wall, leaving a trail of buttery yellow. Henry's humming something too low to make out, and after a moment he pushes the ladder further down so he can reach where the wall meets the cavernous ceiling.

I put aside the book I hadn't been reading and consider. "I like it."

"Well, it's your house, ma'am," he says, smile evident in his voice. I watch him in the mirror hanging above the mantle cattycorner to where he's working, a shifting portrait. A swoop of dark hair appears and disappears and reappears as he leans down to dip the brush into the paint can. I look at the clock on the wall: it's past four in the morning.

A pair of insomniacs could easily haunt each other without one of them being dead. I tell myself this. At first it's a joke. It isn't funny. I keep telling myself this.

"I may have another project for you, Henry." He meets my eyes in the mirror, his eyebrows raised. "It might frighten you," I warn.

"Keeping me on my toes." He sticks the paintbrush into his belt loop and crosses his arms. "Hey, you know me, the more disturbing and physically improbable the better."

The cuckoo clock in the kitchen that hacked up blood and viscera on the stroke of midnight had indeed been disturbing. Then there was the painting of my great-aunt on the third floor that had been used as a dartboard by my last ghost that oozed black grime from its eyes and mouth until Henry threw it out. (I found a severed ear near the painting, too, but I kept that part to myself; Henry is too precious an asset to lose to a little repulsion.)

And that had just been what he'd taken care of on Wednesday.

I stand and pace to the other side of the room. I hold my hand before the mirror and point down at the knickknacks spread across the dusty shelf of the mantle. The ladder knocks against the wall and his footsteps creak across the floor.

The crystal circus had been a gift from my grandmother just as the house had, but I'm sick of looking at it. Like alien invaders, a pile of dead beetles and flies have accumulated in between the clowns and the delicately twirling trapeze artists and the elephants standing on their trunks. I would have packed it back safely into its box if the little glass thugs hadn't attempted murder yesterday. It turns out nothing in the house can be harmless.

As though sensing the threatening thoughts, the archer figurine pivots on its miniscule heel and aims an arrow at my head. I duck in time but Henry grunts just behind me.

"Jesus, what is that!" The tiny crystal arrow, dripping blood, hurtles at the wall from midair. Flecks of blood spatter the floor spasmodically; he's flicking blood from his fingers.

"Are you alright?" Already I'm moving toward the kitchen to get the disinfectant.

"No, I'm fine. Just nicked a little, but what in the . . ." He laughs abruptly. "Here's something to write home about. I'm being intimidated by some antique trinkets." The elephant stands on its hind legs and the dancer posed on its back flips onto its feet on the mantle top, tiny fists raised in a boxer's stance. "I'm going to take a wild guess and say this is what you're worried about?"

"Oh, not at all." With one motion I swipe the whole set off the mantle and they crash, splintering into thousands of pieces on the hardwood floor. I feel an ache in my neck as it breaks, but nothing more.

The ringleader lands on its feet, fists raised to the sky. I crush him under my boot and he gives with a delicate crunch.

"Oh . . ." Because he's a softy Henry's a little taken aback to see any sentient thing destroyed so easily, but then he's a young ghost. He'll learn someday.

I pry up the loose ledge of the mantle and heave it onto the floor. It stirs up a satisfying amount of plaster dust.

"This is your project. Hold your breath. Look inside."

There's a deep intake of breath to my right and then a frantic gurgling. He's choking, and then–

"The very bones of the house are mine, you see. And they could be yours."

I gazed out of the window. She'd sat me down in the velvet window seat in her bedroom and she glowed faintly in the sunlight, her gray eyes were pale but sharp. Her hand on mine was icy and only distinguishable from a skeleton's by a membranous, wrinkled layer of skin. Down in the garden, old Maxwell tore the weeds from the ground and flung them over his shoulder, his mouth working as he whistled to himself. His hair had fallen out in such a perfect circle he could have been mistaken for a monk.

The house, a sprawling Victorian monster from the outside, was only a front for something . . . else. Something primordial, it sits on a hill between an idyllic meadow and a freeway and sometimes attracts tourists who mistake it for a historical site. They don't stay long, but they don't leave, either. Sometimes the house must go into hiding if enough missing people crop up in short enough a time.

As a child, I loved this house. Loved it covetously. It was mine, would be mine. You shouldn't chastise me too harshly.

I pressed my ear to the floor and heard my own heartbeat echoed back and mistook that for love.

"Are you listening to me?"

I nodded, my forehead bumping against the clouded glass. Her grip tightened until her claws sank into my wrist. I only refrained from crying out because I knew what would happen if I did.

"I'm a very old woman, Nora, and very soon I'm going to need you to take over for me. Will you do that? Would you like to?" Her voice quivered feverishly, near tears. She seemed half afraid of me, even as she clutched my arm so hard she drew blood. I'm not sure she was aware of what she was doing.

If she'd asked just a few years earlier when I'd been more naïve I would have leapt to please and obey her.

"You used to throw parties," I whispered.

There had been lavish parties once. My grandmother didn't have wrinkles then, and her hair had shone black as obsidian in the light from the chandelier. I'd been a favored pet, and she'd let me trail after her skirts as she greeted guest after guest after guest. I didn't know any of them but they always seemed happy to see me.

I never saw any of them leave.

To a stranger, she was a charming host, able to turn her affable hostess persona on instantaneously. But she wasn't moving from room to room to chat with her guests; she was prowling. When the person she was speaking to turned away her lip would curl and her hand on the back of my neck squeezed just a little too tight. A mildly sour smell emanated from her in those moments, her intense jealousy of anyone being in the house.

Once, when I was nine, the festivities were coming to an end and I was sent to bed. Every night I was expected to drink a tall glass of milk my grandmother would pour for me and she'd eyeball me until it was all gone. But it made me sleepy, and I'd always vomit into a potted plant when she wasn't looking so I could stay awake until the end of the night. There was no one left on the stairs and no one in the second-floor hall, so I turned and tiptoed back the way I had come. The floor jumped beneath my feet and I decided to follow the distant pulse of music to the basement.

The door swung open and a wall of rotten heat struck, sending me sprawling onto my back. I sat up and could see a red glow like the inside of an oven. The stench of burning meat made me wretch, my stomach already upset from forcing myself to throw up the milk. I started to crab walk backwards when something seized my ankle.

I looked down and saw a devil. Pale flesh oozed from its face. A diamond earring fell by my foot, still pinned to a melting earlobe. Its red mouth opened and closed spasmodically, like a balloon rapidly deflating and the sound of a distant thunderstorm rumbled from its chest. Its eyes were white tears.

"Hehhhh," it said to me as it died. "Hehhhhhh."

I kicked the burning woman away from me. Someone was screaming and screaming and screaming and I knew nothing except a wave of fire rising from the basement stairs to claim me along with the hundreds of bodies below.

My grandmother's heels clicked close to my ear. The door was shut with a matter-of-fact crunch of bone.

"You're up past your bedtime," my grandmother said in a disinterested tone, pulling the combs from her long hair and shaking it loose over her shoulders. "Well, you were going to learn eventually, honey. The house has to feed now and then." She patted my head as she passed, leaving me there on the floor, panicked and scrubbing at the scorching secondhand skin pasted to my ankle.

The woman's hand had broken off on the door and lay palm-up, fingers curled inward, a dead tarantula.

The next I knew I woke up in bed. The first thing I did was fly down the stairs and look into the basement, but there was no lingering smell of charred flesh or smoke and everything looked as it always had.

Except the inside of the door was riddled with claw marks.

"Yes, I threw parties once," my grandmother said that cold afternoon in the window seat. "And what of it?" She took my hand and held up a skeleton key, three identical teeth gleaming dully in the light. "That's just a trial of living as we do, of bearing the name le Roy. Don't you want to own the house? It's the highest honor I'm giving you, something passed down through the generations in our family. You could live forever, Nora. You won't be ungrateful, will you? I didn't raise you to be a brat who couldn't recognize a good thing when she saw it."

I hesitated.

Her familiar mask vanished. She got very close to my ear and hissed, "Don't you want to own the house? Would you like to? Don't you want to be the house? Would you like to? Would you like to? Would you —"

"Yes!" I cried, anything to get away from this woman I no longer recognized.

Before I could jump away, she took my hand and pressed the key into it. It sizzled, white-hot, so hot that for a moment it was cold, a nothing-sensation, and then smoke trickled from my palm and I screamed just as it was over.

My grandmother was gone. But I watched the image of my grandmother as she'd been as a young woman walk past her vanity mirror. She was tying her black hair into a knot with smooth hands.

"Very good of you, dear," her voice said from by the door. "I knew you were the stupidest of your sisters. That's why I chose to keep you for myself, why your mother and father agreed to it. If you weren't an idiot, you would have ran while you still could. I wouldn't have stopped you."

The door opened and shut. Her footsteps retreated, feather-soft on the hallway carpet.

With a jolt of cold sparks licking up my spine, I felt the front door bolt shut. It was like a phantom limb, this newfound tendril of power, and behind my eyelids I watched my grandmother tug at the door, becoming frantic and throwing herself at it. Her eyes rolled around in her head like a prey animal knowing the teeth sinking into its neck are killing it but still struggling to free itself –

The first floor exploded in fire.

I looked out the window. Blind and deaf Maxwell Paterson, the good-natured butler who had worked for my grandmother since before I came to the house and never looked directly at me or seemed to hear me, now looked up and went running to where flames waved from the windows, red arms flailing for help.

He heaved the front door open and my grandmother fell at his feet, still clinging to life but barely, twitching, still very much on fire.

Maxwell ran back for the hose and did what he could. He sat with her propped in his lap, holding her hand as she slipped away.

He peered into the house from the open doorway. There was no fire that he could see.

He looked at my grandmother, really looked at her with eyes that could see all along, as though he'd never seen her before.

"Who *are* you?" he said, but she didn't answer.

I rolled the key around, around in my hand.

Maxwell was the first ghost. He tried to leave in the night a week later after police took my grandmother's body away. The front door collapsed on him. He was found still clutching the doorknob.

I come as close as I can to touching his shoulder and hold up the key.

"You have to kill it, Henry."

Inside the hollow space in the mantle beats a heart gushing blood from a tear in its side. It doesn't appear to be connected to anything.

His hand hovers over the key but he doesn't take it. "But . . . whose . . . why?"

"Because it's . . ."

Henry's eyes are wide in the mirror. The color of truth, the daunting question: *What are you?*

"It's mine. And it'll kill you if you don't."

After Maxwell there was Amie who'd had strawberry-blonde hair, a paranoid disposition, and who'd lasted under a month. She cursed the silence on the other end of the rotary phone and paced the first floor like a caged animal, twisting to throw frantic looks over her shoulder, at the stairs, even up at the ceiling. She shuddered at the smiling cherubs painted there. The house was ready to spit her out soon after that, her chronic terror unpalatable. She didn't get farther than grabbing her dusty car keys.

I watched as the curtains my grandmother kept in the parlor to hide the setting sun lurched from the windows and seized Amy's throat.

At the very least, it didn't take long.

Armin was the ghost of a waif, might have been ten or a gruesomely underfed seventeen. He had been a runaway, from what I could gather, and was just looking for a warm place to rest for a while. He slept curled in a little ball on the hearth like a cat, and the next morning he ventured into the west wing. I tried to stop him, I . .

His screams bounced around the walls for a few hours and then it was quiet again. I kept my eyes pinned to the road from the window and prayed for solitude.

Then there was Mr. Tuffy, which wasn't his real name. He wore a permanent scowl and if I hadn't known better I would have been sure the house wouldn't take him. His demeanor was too gruff, and he didn't care much about the house. He disappeared often and was rarely around, and when he was he kept mostly to the newer side of the house, namely the kitchen. He'd make coffee, black no sugar, and sit at the table and glare at the newspaper, and that was all I'd see of him all day.

Everything was going well, if a bit uneventful, until he got it in his head to tear the bathroom wall down on the second floor. A wooden beam struck him between the eyes and that was that for Mr. Tuffy.

And then there was my final ghost, who found the cobwebs tangled over the front entry charming.

"Hoo boy," he said, swiping away a tarantula-sized fly inches from his face. The stupid man was smiling. "They weren't kidding about the Addams Family."

He'd set his suitcase down and slowly began looking around the room, his boots loud on the marble floor. His gaze passed the mirror and snapped back to it; his eyes met my reflection.

"Hey!" He spun around but of course there was nothing to be seen. When he looked back at the mirror I was gone, cowering in the corner against the wall. "It's alright," he said, lowering his voice in the soothing way one talks to a frightened child. "I'm just here to clean up the house, yeah? I answered your ad in the paper?"

"This is my house," I said. The windows rattled in their frames. An antique plate fell from the wall. "This is my house."

"I know, I know. Hey, lady, I'm here to help. Can you come back where I can see you?"

After a long pause, I stepped back in view of the mirror.

He had a dreamy look about the eyes, as though he wasn't firmly rooted in reality, which I supposed, neither had I been, not for a very long time. He hitched the strap of his bag further up his shoulder and took a step closer, his hand reaching out to the mirror. In the reflection, he appeared to be right behind me.

"I'm Henry," he said quietly. "I'm the cleaning guy."

I knew this already. I had placed the ad in the paper, had replied to his phone call nearly catatonic with relief. It had been decades since my last ghost and the house was starving.

"I'm Nora."

"You didn't mention you were a ghost, Nora," he said. "I mean, no offense. I think that's totally righteous."

I didn't correct him. I wanted to be righteous. God help me, I wanted to be righteous.

He's been here for nearly a year now. In that time the house hasn't devoured a soul, hence its restlessness, the circus set, the painting, the clock. It's slowly dying, but it's going to kill us both first.

"I can't do it myself, Henry." I'm begging now, I'm trying to press the key into his hand. "You have to do it. You have to."

"You're a ghost," he says sadly.

"I know." And I do. I've been dead since 1902 when my grandmother led me through the front door.

I guide his hand to the mantle. It feels like touching a pocket of warm air.

"Your name is Henry le Roy. Do you know what that means?"

"Well . . . Well, I don't know. I think Henry means—"

"It means this house should go to you by all rights. You're next in line. The moment you take this key it will be yours. It will be you. You're not going to take the key, Henry."

Below the mantle, quicker than the debilitated house can react, I ignite the fire.

"Go on, Henry. For your sake and mine, for everyone."

Henry stares into the fire. His eyes reflect the flames. He looks up at me pitifully.

He says, "We won't get to hang out anymore."

I laugh, perhaps for the first time in my life.

"No. No, we won't. That's alright. It's enough."

He takes the key.

I look down at myself, at the veins in my hands, the bloodstains on my ninety-year-old dress. I can no longer see Henry, but the key flips through the air into the fire.

It's instantaneous.

A panicked scream, the whistle of a teakettle set to boil, issues from all corners of the room, from the base of the house itself. Is it mine? Does it matter?

The heart, the house's heart and mine, sprays a weak arc of blood into the air. The roof quakes and falls aside with an earth-shaking groan. The walls melt, rippling like a mirage.

My only comfort is Henry, that Henry is, will be . . .

Faintly now, I see his edges, an afterimage of the young man. He bends over the hearth, intent on the fire. His hands pass through it unaffected.

He plucks the key out of the ashes and holds it up in the light exposed by the collapsed walls.

"You were too good, Nora," he says. "Too soft. I saw the scars on your hand."

He clutches the key in a bony hand.

"It doesn't burn me at all. A tool of the gods recognizes its master."

Henry stuffs the key into his pocket and steps over my fallen form, humming a song of war.

The house begins to burn.

Amanda Hemphill

Growing up, Amanda Hemphill wanted to go to space and
 travel to fantasy worlds, but since she learned there are no fantasy worlds and she never grasped simple math, she decided to write about other worlds instead. She was born and raised on the Eastern Shore of Virginia, where she lives and writes to this day. When she is not being a student, she is working on a novel.

The Vampire's Kiss
By Dorian T. Chase

The woman walked down the shadowy street lit by lamplight, and the vampire watched from those shadows. She wore only a simple, brown dress, but he decided that she was without a doubt the most beautiful woman he had ever seen. Her hair was tied up with a modest blue bow. Her skin was milky white, and her features were supple and delicate. The vampire wanted her more than he had ever wanted anything in his entire life.

From the moment he had seen her two hours prior, he had followed her in secret. He did not understand why he did so. He had simply been looking for a meal. She was not the first pretty women he had met in the night. He'd usually kill a woman of her caliber without a second thought, but never before had he felt such a powerful surge of want and desire.

The vampire grimaced; this was taking precious time away from his hunting. As the night grew, it would become increasingly difficult to find someone to feed on. The drunks would be stumbling home, one by one. The prostitutes would be turning in with rich gentlemen to please for the night. As each moment passed, the vampire would have less prey.

Still, he could not peel his eyes away from this beauty even for a moment. Why was she out here this late? What was she doing? She was not like the typical whores and tramps that prowled the streets at night. They all had a distinct smell. It was harsh to his sensitive nose. Instead, this woman smelled lightly of a bouquet of flowers. He could not tell if her smell was a concoction of some perfume, or if she handled the flowers herself. Either way, it only served to enhance her charm.

He hid in the shadows, sneaking from dark alley to hidden crevice. He knew his appearance would terrify anyone who saw him, so hiding had become like an art form to the vampire. He was adept at moving in silence and stepping to avoid the refuge that built up in the alleyways. He always used the wispy fog and poor lighting to his advantage.

For the alluring woman's benefit, she stuck to the well-lit, well-paved areas and kept her high-heeled shoes grounded, never slipping or missing a step. She moved quickly with a confidence that she knew where she was going.

She is so graceful. The vampire mused.

He had met so few people who ever exuded grace. Perhaps that was why he had given up his own grace so long ago.

A beggar stumbled out of a nearby alley and the vampire barely stopped himself from surging forward. The drunken homeless man looked like trouble. The vampire wanted more than anything to leap out into the light and pull the imperfection staining his view away. Only this woman deserved to be in his sight.

"Change?" The beggar stumbled towards her with an outstretched hand.

The vampire had expected her to turn away in revulsion. The woman should have given him a look of disgust and stormed off. She should have slapped the drunken old man to the ground. She should have turned around and run. However, she did none of these things. Instead, she went into her purse and pulled out a single silver coin. She grabbed the drunkard's arm and placed the coin into his hand, closing his fingers around it.

She gave him a smile. The vampire found that smile intoxicating. It was exactly the kind of smile he would have imagined she possessed. It was beautiful like her.

The woman turned away. The drunk man grabbed her arm and the vampire tensed. It took every ounce of will that he had not to reveal himself right then and there. However, he had not lived a hundred years by being reckless.

The homeless man's hands were grimy. The vampire's enhanced night vision could tell that the old man was leaving smears of dirt on her beautiful dress. However, the beautiful woman was not afraid. She gently rested her hand on the beggar's arm and continued to smile.

The beggar suddenly seemed surprised at his own actions, and a little embarrassed at his outburst. He let go of her dress, and she gently guided his hand to her bosom, holding the grimy hand with both of hers. Then, she leaned forward and kissed the man on the forehead. The vampire stifled back a gasp followed by a surge of anger and frustration that he didn't understand.

The old beggar grinned with a toothy smile. "Thank you, m'lady."

The man backed off a few steps, bobbing his head almost comically while offering her more than adequate room to advance. She nodded at him with her gorgeous smile and then continued to glide forward with that wonderful grace of hers. The vampire bit back the desire to kill the beggar and instead continued to follow the woman.

He realized that the rage he felt was simple jealousy. The beautiful woman had given a man as dirty and as ugly as the vagrant a kiss simply for being himself. If she was the kind of woman who could do that, would she be the kind of woman who could give the vampire her love as well? He briefly imagined her kissing him, accepting him despite his scarred and rough features. He might have blushed if he had blood in his veins.

She turned abruptly, walking up the steps to a small house and knocked on the door. After a moment, the door swung open revealing a middle-aged woman on the other side. She greeted the vampire's new love excitedly. They hugged, and then the woman of his affection entered the house.

Had she finally made her way home? The vampire began to panic. He was not done seeing her yet. He had not decided what he wanted to do. He wondered how she would taste. He wondered if she would reject him. He needed to know more about her. He desperately looked around for a way to see her again and noticed a small cracked-open window in front of the brick house.

Carefully working his way across the street, he snuck under the windowsill, using a nearby bush to conceal himself. After a moment of listening carefully, his found he could make out voices. They came from another room, but he was close enough that he could pick up some words.

"It has been a long time since you last came here. Look how you've grown!" an older woman exclaimed.

"Thank you, Mrs. Goodsprin. I know my father has been meaning to write," another woman responded.

That voice was melodic; it could only have come from the vampire's love. He stifled a sigh, letting the voice of his love caress his motionless heart.

"Oh, don't be silly," Mrs. Goodsprin was saying. "But it is good to see you. The last time I saw you, Veronica, you were only about yay tall."

Veronica? Was her name Veronica? The name fit her like a glove. It was easily as beautiful as she. He wanted to say the name out loud. He wanted to let the words caress his lips, but he dared not make a sound.

"But either way," Mrs. Goodsprin continued after saying something the vampire must have missed, "Why are you out this late? It's not safe at night."

"I stay to the light and populated areas of town," Veronica defended herself. "Also, my father insisted that this be delivered to you at once."

"What's this then?" the vampire could hear the rustling as if wrapping was being torn off of something. "Oh my, that is lovely! Still, dear, you shouldn't have risked yourself for something like this; it really could have waited until it was light out."

"Then I wouldn't have been the one to deliver it," Veronica mused, "I really wanted to see the look on your face."

"Oh dear, well tell your father I love it, and thank you for this." Mrs. Goodsprin sighed. "It really has been a long time."

"Well, as you mentioned it is late and I really should be on my way," Veronica explained.

"So soon? Can't you stay for a while longer? My husband should be coming home soon. He'll be able to walk you home safely."

"I'm sorry. My father's on a deadline and I need to be there to assist him."

Mrs. Goodsprin said her farewells with Veronica. The door opened and the vampire made sure to back into the fog and shadows once again. Mrs. Goodsprin made one more attempt to keep Veronica until her husband could escort her home. When Veronica politely declined, the vampire let out a sigh of relief. The Goodsprin woman was quickly getting on his nerves. He wanted Veronica alone to himself.

As Veronica strode down the street, the vampire moved to follow her once again. He really was running out of time. It was already close to midnight. Once again, he found himself wondering how she tasted. He imagined she tasted wonderful, a combination of the flowers in her scent and the sweetness of her soul. Then he stamped down those thoughts. If he fed on her, he would struggle to control himself. Either he'd kill her, or she would run in terror. Either way would end any chance he had of ever seeing her again.

Perhaps there was another way? The vampire could always change her. He had never changed someone into a vampire like himself. His sire had perished a long time ago, and they had only spent a few brief years together before a mob had caught up with the pair of them. The vampire's sire had been a gentle and kind master, and before he died he had explained to the vampire what it would take to sire someone else. In essence, a vampire must drain the person of blood, and then leave a drop of his own blood in their mouth. It seemed easy, but he had never done it before and feared he could kill her rather than change her.

Either way, Veronica would be home soon. That would eliminate any chance of him doing anything. Of course, he could always break into her room at night, but that was never his way. Experience told him that kind of act riled up the townspeople too much. A girl out at night suddenly going missing was a common occurrence. A girl swept from the comforts of her own room meant a mob.

Would he even want to turn this beautiful creature before him into something like him? How could she fare as a nightwalker? Would the thought of having to feed and kill and being surrounded by blood and death entice her or disgust her? He imagined the beggar again, and tried to contemplate how she would respond to the disgusting world he could introduce her to. Would she smile at it and embrace it, like she did with that drunkard? Or would embracing that culture break the woman he had fallen in love with.

After a few more moments of contemplation, he finally made his decision. He broke his sight away from her for a bit as he ducked down another alley. Even those few moments of being unable to see her felt miserable, but he needed to get ahead of her if he was to carry out his plan. He moved with an unnatural speed from alley to alley, leaping over trash, fences, and other obstacles with skill.

After a few minutes, he positioned himself in an alley that Veronica had yet to reach. He crouched down in the shadows, waiting for the moment to pounce. That moment didn't come. After a minute or two passed, he became agitated. It was a risk. He knew he was being impatient, but he had to look. He took a quick glance out into the street.

Veronica was not there. Panic began to set in. Where was she? Did she forget something and suddenly turn around? Did she decide to take some alleyway route he did not predict? Was he so unlucky that her house was between the point he left her eyesight and the alley he prepared the ambush?

He walked out into the cobblestone street, into the light. It was something he did not do often, but he needed a clearer view. He raced down the street, following the path that Veronica should have walked. He listened carefully, hoping to hear the clicking of his love's high-heeled shoes on the rocky ground.

He could hear a sharp sound off in the distance. It was a woman's cry; he instinctually recognized Veronica's voice. The noise came from an alleyway, one that the vampire had bypassed when he went to head her off. He could hear other noises as well, there were men present and it sounded like she was in a struggle.

The vampire suppressed a surge of fear and began running. Why had he left her out of his sight? He had been so foolish. Of course, he wouldn't be the only danger on a night like this.

The vampire slid into the alley, quickly trying to assess the situation. Veronica was on the ground, her dress was torn and there was a group of men standing around her. One of the men looked to be trying to force her to the ground. Two of the other men were standing, each brandishing sharp-looking knives. The vampire growled at the sight. There was a bruise on Veronica's arm. How dare they tarnish his perfect Veronica?

The men must have noticed the growl and turned around. In the darkness of the alley, they could not make out any of the vampire's features. If they had, they might not have been so careless. The man on the ground concentrated on keeping Veronica from running, while the other two turned to the vampire.

"Well, well, what do we have here? A good Samaritan hoping to save a damsel? Well sod off, if you know what's good for you!" one of the men spat.

"He's seen our faces." the other man whined nervously. "We can't let him live."

The two men descended on the vampire. The first man lunged, and the vampire easily avoided the thrust of his knife. He grabbed the man's neck and twisted, causing a sickening crack. The vampire allowed the man to collapse to the ground. The nervous man squeaked, suddenly finding himself alone.

The vampire took an intimidating step towards the man. The coward slashed the knife at him while jumping back. The vampire casually took a step back, easily avoiding the swipe.

"Stay away," the man threatened, his voice tinged with fear as he waved the knife without any form.

The vampire took a step forward again and the man swiped the knife again. This time, the vampire allowed the blade to strike through his skin, and then closed the distance between himself and the brute. The vampire rammed his hand into the man's abdomen, piecing the skin. The would-be rapist let out a gasp before his body went slack, blood leaking from his mouth. The vampire pulled the knife from the man's hand before pulling his own hand out of the man's abdomen. He fell to the ground, joining his friend.

The third man finally let go of Veronica, staring in fear at his two fallen comrades. In the darkness of the alley, the vampire imagined the last rapist couldn't see exactly what he had done, but the man knew he had killed his two armed friends in seconds. The last man let out a shout, turning and running away. The vampire considered following him and finishing the job, but his sweet Veronica was right there in front of him.

She unsteadily got to her feet, trying to brush off the mud and dirt. It was far too late for that now. Her hair was a complete mess, and her dress was covered in filth. The strap of her dress was ripped, causing it to fall lower than she had intended. This destroyed a lot of the modesty that she had tried to maintain. The beauty that she had radiated for so long had been sullied by those despicable men.

"You saved me," Veronica's voice cracked but still sounded as beautiful as ever. "Thank you."

The vampire nodded, still, a bit stunned that she was actually talking to him, and not fleeing in terror. His hand still dripped, covered in the blood of the man he had impaled only moments before. She must not have seen what he had done. It was likely that she could not see his face in this dark alley as well.

"Thank you so much!" her façade broke down, tears breaking out as she raced towards him, slamming into him with a deep embrace.

This stunned the vampire further. The woman he loved was hugging him. She was as incredible and as beautiful as he imagined. As she continued to hold him, weeping into his shoulder, he steadily moved his hands around her waist. She accepted them and did not make any movement of protest. She really did tolerate him for whom and what he was.

No, that was not true. He saw the red blood from his arm seeping into her dress. She had not seen what he looked like. Through her tears and her haste, she had assumed he was some valiant knight, not some monster. Soon, she would pull away from this embrace. She would see his face. She would scream, and then she would run.

The vampire had no other choice. She was crying, and he couldn't let her cry anymore. He couldn't let her be afraid anymore. He wouldn't let her be hurt, or have her beauty destroyed by others. He sank his teeth into her neck. Veronica gasped in pain as his teeth lanced into her flesh. She momentarily tried to push away, but he held her tight. He began to gently suck on her neck, drinking the sweet nectar from within her.

Her crying had stopped, and after a moment her eyes closed, her jaw becoming slightly slack and her lips parting just a bit. It was already too late. It was the effect of a vampire's bite. It caused humans to fall into a state of euphoria. It was very personal, very calming, and very addicting. The vampire knew that if he pulled away from her now, she would become an addict.

For the rest of her life, Veronica would chase after him, begging him to bite her neck again and again. She would want that euphoric feeling. That would be all she would think about, all she would live for. And if the vampire didn't provide her what she wanted, she would find another vampire who would. She would slowly waste away, her neck filled with scars, her life empty and meaningless. Whatever beauty she once had would be gone.

The vampire had seen this effect in ghouls before. The bite inevitably always broke the person who was bitten. The only real choices were to kill them by draining all of the blood or turn them into a vampire. Veronica moaned gently as he continued to suck. This sent shivers up and down the vampire's spine.

He had fed and killed many people in his life, but never before had it felt so personal and so close as it did right now. Veronica was sweet. The taste of her was unlike anything he had ever tasted before. The inner soul of her being could be tasted in her blood, and the vampire found what he already had suspected. She was perfect. He began to suck harder.

Veronica's moans became sharper as he bit at her neck more aggressively, sucking every drop from her veins. After a few moments, the moans started quieting, a little bit at a time. When they finally stopped, Veronica became still. The last drop hit the vampire's tongue. He let out a sigh, gently lowering Veronica down on the ground in a dry space. Veronica wasn't dead yet. It was a state between life and death. It was the moment the vampire had waited for. She could die as a perfect beauty, or live the rest of her life as a monster like him.

He lifted his hand up over Veronica's mouth, holding the knife he had taken up to his palm. His hand shook uneasily for the first time that he could remember. He didn't want to be alone anymore. Her skin was already growing cold. Her milky white skin was steadily starting to take on a glossy look. Tears started to full down his cheeks as he trembled over her, afraid to move forward, afraid to step back.

Do it. You're running out of time! The vampire's mind screamed.

A sudden flash of light from a lantern hit the vampire's eyes just as the dagger scratched at his palm. He hissed, looking up at the source that had destroyed his night vision and interrupted his time with Veronica. He pulled away standing up in a hurry. As he glanced down, he could no longer make out Veronica's features in the darkness. Had he done it? He didn't know.

"Hey!" a husky male at the base of the alley shouted.

It appeared to be a night patrolman. The vampire had been careless. He had made too much noise. He'd been too enraptured in what he was doing with Veronica. However, he had no choice but to flee now. If he was found out, both he and Veronica would be beheaded and burned as monsters. He growled, jumped to his feet, and ran, following the same path the would-be rapist had taken to escape earlier. He could hear the patrolman approaching as he ran off, but the man stopped when he reached Veronica.

"What is it?" another man called at the entrance of the alley as the first one bent down to check on the young girl.

The first man sighed and shook his head. The woman had a little bit of blood resting on her lips. He wiped the blood off and closed her eyes. Upon standing, he peered down the dark alley just as the vampire turned a corner, disappearing once again into the shadows.

"Nothing we can help now." The other man sighed. "Just another monster of the night."

Dorian T. Chase

Dorian T. Chase is a student at Wright State University. He writes fiction which he publishes at

www.wattpad.com/elementalcobalt, justanotherscienceguy.com, and on Amazon. He currently has two self-published novels on Amazon, Bad Boys of Fairmont High and Bad Boys in Space! He specializes in humor, science fiction, fantasy, and the

supernatural.

A Small Town
By Kelly Doyle

When we were kids, my brother fell off his bike and skinned his elbow two houses down; my mother received three calls before he picked himself off the pavement. When a yellow hand shovel was stolen out of our neighbor's yard, the town newspaper voiced our collective indignation until it was found, misplaced underneath the owner's deck. It was a seven minute drive from our little brick house to Hawkins' grocery store. I passed the only school I had ever attended. I passed my parent's house, which looked exactly like mine except for the pink flowers out front. I passed the movie theater, the pharmacy, the dollar store. I passed the park where my mother used to let me swing and where I would one day take my daughter, Izzy, once she was old enough. Just about everything fit into that little space. Nothing happened without everyone knowing and it was easy to spot trouble. I had always felt comforted knowing I was part of a system that made sense. But things were different now and I resented it, watching these familiar places pass outside my window on the way to Hawkin's grocery store. I hadn't been to Hawkins' in a year and a half and I wouldn't have been going at all if the other grocery store in town hadn't closed down for lack of customers.

"It's closing?" I exclaimed when Frank told me over the breakfast table a few weeks earlier. "What do you mean? Why?"

"There just aren't enough people to support two grocery stores," he replied, taking another sip of coffee and flipping to the next page of the newspaper. "Why would they stay here when they can move?"

"But…" I pushed down the top so he would look at me, "why didn't *Hawkins'* close?"

"Not everyone has kept up this little boycott of yours," he replied with a sigh.

"Well, I'm still not going." I crossed my arms. Frank looked at me. We did not often disagree. There was a tense moment before he returned to his reading, but two weeks later the pantry was empty and Frank was at the end of his rope.

"Just go," he said.

"I don't want to. Especially not with Izzy." I waited nervously for his reaction, bracing myself for whatever was to come.

"You used to go all the time."

"That was before *she* worked there."

"She might not even be there. You'll be fine."

"I don't want to be near her. She's trouble."

"So ignore her, Mary Beth!" He stood up from his chair so that he was leaning over me. I didn't like it when he used my name.

"We need food and I sure as hell ain't gonna go. That's your job. You're the mother."

I finally conceded, only because all I had ever wanted to be was the perfect mother and I hated making Frank mad. But the next day, standing in front of the glass doors gripping my grocery list against the handle of my cart, I regretted the decision. Chicken, bread crumbs, olive oil, oregano and milk. That was all I needed to appease Frank for another day or two. Izzy bounced happily in the cart, totally unaware of the emotions roiling in my stomach. "All right," I said aloud, "let's go." I started towards the entrance. The glass doors opened automatically when I approached and a little bell rang.

"Morning!" Tom called from the only register. I glanced his way and there she was, Molly Hawkins, standing beside him with her hair in two dark plaits on either side of her head. My stomach gave a jolt. She was still so young. She must have been, I thought for a moment, seventeen now. She was seventeen.

I couldn't believe it had been over a year since the trial, over a year since Molly Hawkins had stabbed and killed her father in the kitchen of their single story home. "In the neck with a steak knife," Sandy Hastings had told me at book group. Usually I ignored her gossip because I had inevitably already heard it or been there when it happened, but this time, when I leaned across the table with an open mouth, she recognized the invitation to continue. "Blood everywhere." She took a sip of her wine and I remember feeling nausea rise up into my throat as I watched the red liquid slosh around her cup and meet her lips.

I walked quickly past the girl with Izzy bouncing before me. I did not respond to Tom's greeting and turned down the first aisle that I could. Izzy quieted down, as if she could sense my urgency.

I had known Molly's father, Stevie Hawkins. I sat next to him in Biology in the ninth grade. Older than me by three years, he was tall and attractive, but never very smart. His voice was deeper than the other boys and he had a cocky smile that made him popular with students, teachers and parents alike. Stevie's younger brother, Tom, seemed to trail after him like a scrawnier, quieter copy. Tom was thin and sweet but he wasn't like Stevie. He didn't talk like him or walk like him and people didn't notice him the way they noticed Stevie. Stevie got married right after graduation and Molly was born only a few months later. She was close to three when Stevie's wife, I had forgotten her name, left them both and moved out of town. I remember watching from the window of a neighbor's house as she dragged her suitcases across the driveway and shoved them into the back of their station wagon. She drove off before Stevie got home. This was a scandal the likes of which our town had rarely seen. There was talk, of course, but no one really knew why she left. "Poor Stevie," Sandy had said at book group, "a single dad." What a shame, we all agreed. Poor Stevie. A few years later, news came that his ex-wife was mowed down by a biker in New York City. Word was, she smacked her head on the pavement. I heard Molly didn't cry at the funeral.

I maneuvered my way through the aisles, lingering at the end caps where I could not be seen. Each time I passed a gap in the shelves, exposing myself to where she stood, I felt she was looking at me. I kept my eyes straight ahead.

Molly grew up to be thin and pretty with long arms and long fingers but people always said she was quiet and strange, or maybe that just arose after the trial, when everyone said they had seen it coming.

It seemed a very adult crime to me but she was tried as a child. The events became even more disturbing when new evidence was released that she had aborted a baby the previous year, a baby she eventually claimed was due to the unsavory acts of her father. This was too horrible, we all agreed. Too horrible to believe. She's sure to rot in jail, I thought. But, to my utter bewilderment, the jury seemed to soften. She was let off with barely a sentence.

"Stevie was not a good man," Tom said. He and Lisa agreed to take the girl and raise her "as she always should have been raised."

Our town newspaper argued for insanity, but Lisa defended her staunchly. "She is not insane. If Stevie Hawkins had been coming at me the way he was coming at her, I would have done the same. She's as sane as you or me."

I only shook my head at this. Any person who can muster the strength to plunge a knife six inches into their own flesh and blood family deserved to die in prison. She was dangerous, and Tom and

Lisa dumb for accepting her. They did not know what it was like to have a child of their own.

"Can I help you find something?"

I jumped, clutching my heart and swiveling to face the figure behind me. It was Tom. I let out my breath slowly.

"You alright, Mary Beth? You seem a little on edge." He gave me a wry smile and his brown eyes said he knew exactly why this was so. He waited, as if offering me an opportunity to change my expression, laugh, make small talk. I sensed his judgment.

"Bread crumbs," I said, not removing my hand from my chest. "Bread crumbs and olive oil." I followed as he led me to the things I needed, humming to himself and making a point to move slowly. As Tom loaded a gallon of milk into my cart, I finally looked up at the register down the aisle where Molly stood. I stared at her for a moment. She had a cold sort of beauty with pale skin and dark hair. I imagined her then with red dripping from her slender hands. It was the first time I ever looked upon a killer. She turned away, noticing my gaze and appearing almost embarrassed. She fiddled with the register and did not look up again.

"Here." Tom pulled my attention back to the task at hand. I grabbed a pack of chicken, not bothering to check the weight or the price, and hurried to the spices. When I finished, Tom and Molly were both waiting at the register. I placed my things quickly on the conveyor belt and Tom began scanning them one at a time. "How have you been, Mary Beth?" He smiled warmly, "It's been awhile since we've seen each other."

"Fine."

"Did you find everything alright?"

"Yes." I watched as Molly extended one pale hand towards the cylinder of bread crumbs. She saw me watching. As if in slow motion her fingers spread, her hand approached the package and suddenly I cried out, "Stop! I'd rather do my own bagging, if that's alright."

Tom paused, the bottle of olive oil poised over the scanner. "Actually," he said calmly, "that's Molly's job. You've met Molly, right, Mary Beth?" It was as if he was teasing me. "My niece?"

I nodded stiffly even though we had never formally met.

"She can handle it."

The girl's hand curled around the cylinder and a wave of disgust ran through my body. Those hands. I passed Tom a few bills, took my bags on my arms, scooped up my daughter and headed for the door. As I passed, Molly pulled at her braids and sighed.

When we reached the car, I held Izzy in my arms for a few moments before buckling her into her car seat. "Hey, sweetie," I cooed, bouncing her up and down. She pulled her fingers out of her mouth and reached to grab at my hair and my neck. They felt wet on my skin and her nails scratched against my cheek. "Oh," I murmured taking her hands in mine, "we will have to cut those nails. Won't we, sweetie?"

Her buckle clicked as I strapped her into her seat. Then her attention diverted, eyes resting behind me, as if she had caught sight of something. A shadow moved across the side of the car and I heard someone breathe. I turned and Molly loomed behind me. "Get away! What do you want?" I shrieked.

Her black eyes hardened. Surprise and hurt spread across her face then turned into anger. Her lips became tight. I flinched. She raised one long arm and thrust a gallon of milk into my open hands. I had left it sitting in the cart. She made to run back into the store then, but she stumbled and fell onto the pavement with a smack. I stepped forward somewhat unsteadily as she pulled her knee up towards her face, staring at its pink surface where skin used to be.

"Are you all…?"

"Stay back," she said furiously, wiping tears from her cheeks. It was the first time I had heard her speak in person. "Don't help me. I don't want help from you, not you or anyone like you." She choked on the last word, pulling herself up from the pavement and stumbling into the store where Tom met her in an embrace.

I slammed Izzy's door and climbed into the car, pressing my forehead against the hot steering wheel. I kept seeing Molly's eyes. I only looked up when quiet knocking sounded on the window. Tom stood outside. I rolled down the window reluctantly.

"Mary Beth…" Though he had approached me, he did not seem to know what to say. He looked at his feet and shook his head. "Come back if you want to. You know you're welcome. But if you don't want to…if you're not comfortable…then just…" he shook his head harder, "then just stay away."

I stared at him and said nothing, gripping the wheel so hard my knuckles were white.

Finally he looked up and there were tears in his eyes, too. "I know what you're thinking when you come in here. I can see it in your face. You're not the only one." Still I said nothing. "You have to understand the tragedy. How long will she be thrust from society? Ogled like a zoo animal?"

I let out a huff of air. "You disgust me, Tom," I said. "She killed your brother. Doesn't family mean anything to you? She killed Stevie." I said his name as if we had been more than acquaintances. "She doesn't belong here."

"It's not like that. I won't keep saying it forever. There has to come a point when—"

"This used to be such a nice, little town, Tom."

"It's still the same town."

"No, it's not, not for my little Izzy." I spat. "Everything has changed."

"Mary Beth…"

"If you don't want me to come, I won't." I said, "I'll drive an hour if I have to but I won't pretend I'm blind to the madness." It was then I noticed that Molly had come out of the store. She was standing behind Tom, watching the both of us. A drip of blood trickled down the front of her shin.

He prepared to respond again, but Molly stopped him before he had the chance. "Uncle," she called, "it's okay. Come back in." So Tom turned and put his arm around the girl and they walked away together. He wasn't as skinny as he was in high school but I could still picture him chasing after Stevie, after his big, talented brother. What a mess, I thought. What a terrible mess.

We drove home. That night, I tucked Izzy into bed and, before she fell asleep, I pressed my lips to her cheek. "You love us, Izzy. Don't you?" I said. "You love your father and me?" I waited until she fell asleep, then I went to bed and listened to Frank snore beside me. Frank isn't perfect, I thought, but who is? Who doesn't get mad once in awhile? And Izzy loves us so much. I thought about Molly's eyes until sleep found me.

I didn't go back to Hawkins'. Every other week I drove Izzy out to the next town and I thought about Molly as I searched for my ingredients in the huge chain grocery store that played music too loud. It was strange leaving town, driving from one end to the other and watching the stage of my entire life pass. I had never had any reason to leave before.

Molly reminded me that things could go very wrong in that small space. I couldn't seem to banish the image of her face as she looked up at me from the pavement, clutching her skinned knee, as if she contained chaos. I wanted her to leave our little town before she ruined it forever, move to a big city where mothers carry pepper spray on the subway and can't let go of their children's' hands for fear of something I had never known. Things are dangerous in cities. Not like our little town. Not until Molly Hawkins stabbed her father in the neck.

I made sure I never saw her again.

Kelly Doyle

Kelly Doyle is a student studying creative writing and psychology at Emory University. She has been reading her entire life, from *The Magic Tree House* and *Harry Potter*, to *Wuthering Heights* and *Americanah*. Aside from loving the smell of paper, she has always felt that reading is the simplest way to reach out of the bubble of her

existence and learn to understand, appreciate, and empathize with those who are different than her. It is for this reason that she writes not only her own perspective, but the perspectives she seeks to understand. She takes inspiration from her study of psychology to explore themes such as empathy, identity, and trauma in her stories. Her work has been published in *Firewords Quarterly*, *Glass Mountain*, *Plain China* (pending), and *Alloy Literary Magazine*. This is her second year being published in *Stories through the Ages*. She would like to thank her parents and brothers for their ever present faith and encouragement, and for ordering no less than a hundred copies of every magazine that includes her work.

The Cottage by the River
By Teresa Juarez

Cali sat cross-legged on the kitchen floor. Her back against the refrigerator, a blue plastic bowl sitting on top of her overgrown belly. Jax, was spread out next to her with his head rested on her leg, his ears flopped on top of his head. She felt beads of sweat running down the back of her neck and let out a groan. Jax began to howl but stopped abruptly when the screen door swung open.

"What in the hell are you doing on the floor again?"

"Heat rises. The closer to the ground I am, the cooler it is."

"How long you been here for? Just waiting around for me to help you up?"

Andy removed the bowl from where she had it balanced and set it into the empty sink. With one swift motion, he lifted her to her feet. She wiggled her toes to unstick them from the linoleum. They were achy already, but the sweat from the hot Georgia day made her even more uncomfortable. She sauntered her way out of the door and sought relief in the rocking chair on the back porch. Her grandfather had made it for her grandmother when she was carrying her first child. Cali waddled onto the patio and plopped down against the old wood, shaded by a big blue umbrella.

Andy came through the door with a new bowl, like the one before, except it was purple. It was filled with her favorite mint chip ice cream, drizzled with magic shell chocolate sauce. This was the current addition to the craving of the month club. Her mood-swings overcame her and she began to sob.

"What's wrong doll?"

"I hate that color. It's the worst one."

"No, no sweetie. This one is for me. I would never bring you ice cream in an ugly purple bowl. I don't even know why we have this bowl."

She wiped her eyes and noticed Jax looking up at her. After she gave him a nod, his head rested back down on her bare feet; the soft fur of his ears draped across her toes. That dog was always worried about her and she could tell. He didn't sleep much like most animals did because he was always watching her.

Andy returned with a fresh bowl, plain white this time, in an attempt to avoid another mood swing. She took the spoon and swirled it around in the bowl, to soften the consistency. She let the first bite melt in her mouth slowly. A neighbor's grill was lit and the scent of freshly grilled hot dogs carried through the air and into their yard. Cali fell to her knees and began heaving off of the patio. Andy ran and grabbed her hair with one hand while he stroked her back with the other. Jax jumped up and started barking into the distance, as though he was trying to ward off the evil.

During the next few days, the Georgia heat was at its climax, which kept Cali laying around with the fans on full speed. She became increasingly uncomfortable and increasingly irritable. Andy kept his distance to avoid contributing to her mood swings. He spent most of his days in the workshop on the side of the house. Cali's grandfather had built it himself, and over the years he had collected everything one could need to paint, build cars, and create amazing pieces out of wood. He taught Andy everything he knew about carpentry, a skill that he practiced to create the perfect nursery for his unborn child.

While giving his wife the space that she needed, Andy worked long hours in the shop and then long hours in the home putting everything together. She had no idea that he built all of the baby's furniture himself. He also made several trips to buy all of the supplies that the baby book suggested to have before Ira's arrival.

"Come up here Cali, you need to see this."

She started her way up the steps, followed closely by Jax. She held back the sour in her stomach as the fumes got stronger. Andy said he had been airing the room out, but to her heightened senses it was moot. She reached the top of the staircase to find Andy standing by the door. He didn't take his eyes off of her as she entered. He stood just outside, leaning against the frame.

"Well, do you like it?"

She spun around slowly to observe his work. It had been painted a light teal color with a white trim. She started her way around slowly, intently, but couldn't find a trace of the ugly purple walls that had been underneath. She ran her hand along the texture as she walked around the perimeter of the room. Without a word she ran to Andy and threw her arms around his neck. He picked her up and slowly spun her around, kissing her all over her face as she giggled. Jax began to howl with excitement.

The crib that Andy built stood proudly on the wall across from the window and was filled with baby Ira's first bedding. It was different shades of blues and greens, with cartoon dinosaurs embroidered into it. There was a stuffed Tyrannosaurus propped up against the bars. It had been Cali's when she was a child and had undergone a quick stitch job to replace one of the eyeballs that Jax chewed off.

There was a changing table on the other wall. It sat at the perfect height for Cali and included many shelves that were well stocked with everything they may need for the new addition to their family. The closet also contained shelves that Andy had built, which were also well stocked, much to Cali's delight. There were almost fifty hangers dangling from the closet that held the clothing that he had picked for his boy. Anyone could tell that Andy picked them because most of it was Georgia Bulldog gear. She smiled to herself wondering how much Ira would look like his dad. She remembered the first time her mother-in-law pulled out the photo albums. That was when she knew she wanted to have Andy's blonde and blue-eyed little baby boys.

That night they lay in their bed with all three windows open. It was dark, aside from the moonlight entering and spreading its beam into their room, stopping directly on a painting that Cali's grandfather made, like a spotlight sent from the Cosmos. She focused on it until she drifted off to sleep which in turn caused her to dream of her grandfather. She walked into the workshop to find him painting. She was a little girl again. Her grandpa was a brilliant artist. Often, he could recreate a landscape after just visiting it once. She looked over his shoulder and saw his work; a river running through a section of mountains. There was a cottage in the yard, just next to the river. You could see the back view of a man sitting on a boulder, with a little girl in a dress seated next to him.

"Look papa, it's us"

The next day was Cali's due date. Ira just wasn't ready to come. She was miserable, always sobbing, complaining about her aching feet, and yelling at Andy. He felt helpless because nothing he offered was suitable. She didn't want him to feed her, help her, or even really touch her.

"We all know what happens when you start lovin' up on me, Andy. Better to stay away."

"You aren't the only one who wants that baby out of there. I want my wife back."

Finally, three days later, the labor began. They had been walking very slowly around the neighborhood when she ran behind a bush in laughter.

"What are you doing?"

"I think I just peed myself."

She laughed so hard about it and it puzzled him. He wondered if she realized that this was the moment. He had seen this exact situation in movies so he had been on edge expecting it for weeks.

"Doll, our boy is coming."

He practically had to pick her up and run her home to the truck. She laughed all of the way until they reached the hospital, which changed her mood immediately. The smile was replaced by tears and the laughter was replaced by whimpers of pain. Again, Andy felt helpless. He expected her to continue to push him away, because it was his fault and all. This was different though. She had his hand in a death grip that had him walking at an angle as the nurse wheeled her down the hall and into the delivery room. One epidural, a shot of Pitocin, and thirty hours later it was finally time for Cali to push.

The next hour seemed to flash by Andy. Everything was a haze of lights, loud noises, and the beeping coming from the heart monitor. He snapped to, realizing two nurses were pulling him out of the delivery room. He heard the cries of his newborn baby and the hustle of the medical staff rushing around the room. He sat down in a conveniently placed chair with his elbows leaning onto his knees and took a few long, deep breaths. It occurred to him that he had no idea what was going on, or why he wasn't in the room with his wife. He charged into the room and saw Cali lying there; eyes closed, with an oxygen mask covering her mouth and nose. He looked over his right shoulder and saw a nurse pushing his baby out of the room in a plastic bassinet.

"Cali? What is going on?"

That was all he could manage to get out through his confusion, and before he was again rushed out of the room. This time they brought him down the hall and through a winding set of confusing hallways. He plopped down in a chair although he couldn't sit still. Every few seconds he stood up and looked down the hallways on both sides, looking for a nurse or someone to talk to.. He sat back down hard and searched his mind for answers. Finally, after what felt like an eternity he was approached by someone he recognized. It was his wife's doctor.

"Your baby is doing very well. I'll take you to see her in a minute."

"Her?"

"Sometimes mistakes can happen. Congrats daddy, you have a daughter now."

He thought about how his baby girl would look in the mini Bulldogs Jersey and camouflage. He smiled because it made him think of his wife. She was so glamourous and beautiful and at the same time she was the coolest buddy he ever had. He remembered the time she found some old home movies from her childhood. In one, she was in Kindergarten playing soccer on asphalt in a pink frilly dress. She fell hard and bashed her knee open down to the cap. She took a bandana from her bag, tied it around her leg and kept on playing. That was the moment that he knew he wanted to be the father of her tough, tan, curly haired, big brown-eyed little baby girls.

"Wait doc, how is my wife?"

The doctor looked down at his feet and let out a heavy sigh. That sigh said the words that he couldn't articulate himself. Andy understood but was in complete disbelief. He took off in a mad dash through the hospital, pushing staff and other visitors out of the way until he reached a door that said "exit". Once outside he fell to his knees. The tears felt like acid as they ran down his cheeks.

"God no, please. You can't have my best friend, you can't. What am I going to do without her?"

He needed to be strong for his baby. When he finally headed back through the doors he shook with every step. His throat was dry, and every swallow felt like he was trying to choke down a rock. His vision was fuzzy through his watery eyes as he followed the signs for the nursery. He stopped at a giant window over-looking rows and rows of babies, sleeping peacefully in their bundles. His gaze ended when he immediately recognized her. There she was, little Cali. Just like the pictures he had of his wife as a baby.

∞

The white paint that coated the wrap-around porch was flaked off in patches. The screen door had a creak when it was opened and closed. The big blue umbrella was faded in sections where the sun had bleached it over the years. The rocking chair underneath had cobwebs weaving through the seat and down to the legs. Little Cali sat on the kitchen floor with her back against the refrigerator. Jax lay sprawled out on the floor with his head in her lap. She was eating a grape Popsicle, and as it melted in her hand, Jax reaped the benefits. She started to get a brain freeze, so she reached down and gave the remainder of it to the dog. He turned to her and licked up the trail of purple that she left on her chin. She giggled loudly, a noise that echoed through the kitchen.

Andy ran inside through the front door, still holding the wrench that he was using. His backwards hat was covered in patches of grease. There were several other streaks of the black on his face, arms, and jeans.

"What's going on in here sugar? Whatcha doin' on the floor?"

"It's really hot in here daddy. The floor is nice and cool."

Jax let out a heavy sigh as he returned his head to her lap and shut his eyes. Cali put her hand under one of his ears and flapped it around while she continued to laugh.

"Come with me a moment, I want to show you something"

She stood up and followed her dad out through the screen door. She followed him down the steps, across the dirt driveway and over to his workshop. Inside, Andy's truck sat with the hood propped open. His tool box was pulled in close, and there was a little wooden step stool in line with the front license plate. A few feet from his truck was another, covered in a large tan tarp. It was her mothers, and had sat there collecting dust for six years now. Andy pulled the tarp up over the bed to reveal several boxes that had been placed inside. He pulled down the tailgate and lifted Cali into it before jumping in himself. He motioned for her to sit down as he rummaged through the boxes. She sat with her legs swinging underneath her, Jax closely watching.

When they returned home from the hospital he had removed almost everything from the home. All of the pictures of him and his wife, along with any other thing that reminded him of her. It's not that he wanted to forget her, he just couldn't cope.

"This stuff belongs to your mama."

"God wouldn't let her bring it to her new house?"

"He would have, but she decided to leave it here for you, sweet girl."

She nodded her head in approval as he handed her a framed picture. She recognized her daddy right away, though he was dressed different. He was wearing a black tuxedo with a pink flower pinned to his lapel. His hair was slicked, and he had a giant smile on his face. He had his arms around a beautiful woman in a pretty white dress. She had big curly brown hair and a bright smile.

"Mama had hair like mine."

Andy nodded his head without saying a word. He rummaged through the boxes some more until he found what he was looking for initially. He pulled out the painting that her great- grandpa had created. He looked at it hard for a moment before handing it down to Cali.

"This was your mama's favorite picture"

"Look papa, it's us!"

She pointed to the boulder next to the cottage along the river. There seated was the back view of a man sitting next to a little girl in a pretty dress.

"I guess so."

Teresa Juarez

Teresa was born in San Diego, California. She is one of six children, and the eldest daughter. She moved to Colorado at a young age, where she developed a love for ballet, pageants, and John Grisham novels. At the age of seventeen, Teresa enlisted in the

United States Navy and moved to Pearl Harbor, Hawaii. She began writing more seriously during her little bit of free time on deployment. After her honorable discharge from service, she moved back to Northglenn, Colorado. She started college, pursuing an English degree, and met her fiancé, Danny, on the first day of class. Teresa's biggest inspirations come from her travel, her favorite authors, and her relationship with Danny. She is currently a Junior at the University of Colorado, Denver. Teresa hopes to be an English teacher following graduation.

Order of the Space Zombies (OSZ)
By Mary Marley Latham

Application Cover Letter

Looking back on my life, I think that I was making choices that would overdetermine the eventuality of an undeath with the Order of the Space Zombies (OSZ) even before the OSZ made first contact.

I remember a day in playschool when my teacher, Ms. Terry, told the class to draw a picture of ourselves. At that time, my parents kept my hair very short, I was an active child and, if my hair was long, it would always be matted and tangled. So, my parents kept it cropped short. Because humans still cling to arbitrary and artificial stylings designed to emphasize gender identity and because short hair has been coded "masculine," several of my classmates assumed that I was a boy, though I didn't realize that this was the case. I guess I never really thought about why I had so many friends who were boys while most girls were almost exclusively friends with other girls. In any case, my friend Bruce asked the teacher what she meant," Is the picture supposed to be just us?"

We were kids, and the question was weird in the way kids'
questions tend to be. I think, he was in that phase a lot of little kids
go through where they are really fascinated by genitalia, probably
because adult humans are so obsessed with covering them. Anyway, I
think he must have been in this phase because, Mrs. Terry didn't get
what he was asking which was that he wanted to know if the pictures
should be *just* us, without clothes. I'm sure she said "no" because I
was the only weirdo to draw a naked self-portrait. I must have
misunderstood, but I really thought she had said "yes" and, being a
kid without a sense of body shame, never questioned the logic. I
suspect her answer may have been overly diplomatic and left room
for confusion. Human children get confused easily, right? Anyway, I
drew a naked picture of myself with a V between the legs, and
suddenly my secret—the secret that I didn't know I had—was out.

I had almost finished the picture when Mrs. Terry walked by.
She was pretty weirded out, but, to her credit, she basically just told
me to fix it. Something about her emotional expression told me that I
had done something very wrong, though. I tried to erase the V, but
my eraser just smudged the page real bad. Then, I drew a big X over
the V, which just emphasized the genitalia even more. Her
instructions had drawn Bruce's attention, and he was both thrilled
that someone had drawn what he had suggested but also freaked out.
He asked why I had drawn that V-shape, and I said that that was how
I looked. It took him a minute to put it together, but it eventually
dawned on him that I was a girl. Suddenly, I was like a different
person, and he told a bunch of the other kids at recess and most of

my boy friends didn't want to play anymore. I remember feeling nauseous and throwing up in my lunchbox later that day then trying to eat what I had thrown up. It was like I had lost control of my body and was trying to take everything back into it.

It didn't have to be the sex/gender system that did it, human society has so many arbitrary and violently enforced categories for bodies. But, for me, it was sex/gender. This "it" that I'm talking about is a crisis where the security of community between individuals is shown for the fragile thing that it is, and an organism (that would be me) experiences social rejection and isolation. Humans are born very premature and need the support and care of their community for a *really* long time before we can take on even rudimentary self-care. To be rejected by the community, on some vestigial psycho-social level, is to be sentenced to death.

I'm trying to say that, at a foundational level, I have been psychologically prepared to crave assimilation into an indissoluble collectivity. When the OSZ made contact in 2028, I was still in secondary school. Everyone in high school had decided I was totally crazy a long time ago, and I had reflexively adopted a philosophy of radical individualism. While I find my former philosophy a bit embarrassing and hard to explain to other Phobiosophers, I can recognize it as a defensive reaction to the superficial nature of conformity (as opposed to community). Because I thought this way, I was able to suspend my judgment when the undead bodies of innumerable species landed on earth, inviting humanity into the ranks of the post-living and post-planetary.

One guy in my class started carrying a crowbar with him everywhere he went. He said it was to defend himself when the space zombies attacked. This was so crazy to me, but everyone just sort of accepted it. Even the school administrators! They thought the same way, really, even though the official stance of the national government was to maintain open communication and, thus, peace. I mean, on Earth, we weren't even able to create international legal systems that extended, supported, or enforced *human* rights protections to stateless people with any true effectiveness. Most humans thought that was just utopian thinking. There was absolutely no historical, legal, or theoretical precedent for a truly collective consciousness formed from a mass of different species that had abandoned an infinite array of planetary systems to reside not only in statelessness but in (with the exceptions of occasional recruitment missions) the void of space. Underpinning a good deal of human order was an assumption that individual human organisms were assets for power systems, so recruiting a human for collective undeath in the void was argued to be a form of theft in some places. That's because we were owned without being really possessed— possession is a two-way street, after all.

It was amazing to go to college because I finally met other progressive-minded people who didn't automatically hate an entity just because it was constituted from a mass of undead organisms. I even made contact with OSZ organisms in my work as a yoga instructor—all the stretching is apparently helpful in preventing the onset of rigor mortis (yoga is a practice that I hope to bring to the

OSZ hive mind if my application is approved). People had so many stupid ideas about the OSZ back then. I mean, people actually thought that the OSZ would try to "infect" the whole human population like in those bigoted movies from the olden days. As if a collective consciousness would want to integrate just any old mind!

So many people are still ready to believe the most ridiculous ideas about the OSZ—mostly based on old myths that are clearly just narratives evolved from archaic psycho-social dynamics. But, I suppose that only means that their minds aren't fitted for undead existence in the void. Sadly, that means they are doomed to regular death and what consciousness they have will only be carried through social legacy. The irony is that most humans are primarily driven by a simultaneous fear and attraction to death that undeath resolves. Once you're undead, you simply don't have to worry about dying because you've already done it, and the fear of blinking out of existence as a consciousness is eliminated because you *know* that you will be absorbed into a cosmic collective consciousness. Even if the undead body is destroyed, the collective consciousness retains your contributions—for as long as the collective will exists—which is potentially forever, considering the ever-expanding fleets in an ever-expanding number of galactic systems. Even interdimensional occupation may well be immanent.

I'm not like these small-minded people who think the OSZ represents absolute existential hegemony, and, ever since the OSZ announced that they would review applications for membership, have developed skills that will allow me to contribute to the way of undeath in space. I remember seeing the announcement on the news. I was working in University of State – Podunk cafeteria. At the time, I was a student worker, trying to cover my living expenses while also going to school full time (I could write a whole other essay about how capitalism made the OSZ seem so amazing). Then, there was a breaking news story, and I learned that humans, if they were willing to prepare their minds and bodies for the change, could become space zombies. I couldn't wait to end my shift and go to the website to read more about it. Every major professional and academic choice I have made since then has been calculated to make me an ideal candidate for induction into the Order of the Space Zombies. I specialized my yoga instruction to optimize mortified bodies, learned all I could about piloting air-and-space crafts, underwent years of psychotherapy, and became passionately interested in Phobiosophy—especially Critical Certainty.

It was through Critical Certainty that I came to more fully appreciate the value of existence that is not only undead but also extra-terrestrial. It's important for organisms to overcome the grounding fallacy. I mean, there may be mostly emptiness in space, but the so-called "ground" of Earth is just a thin layer of soil and rock floating on molten lava. Better to drift eternally than to burn up instantly. Death is the only certainty, but the OSZ has shown humanity that death can mean so much more than we ever imagined. It can be a passage into not just some unprovable fairy-tale of a spiritual afterlife; it can be a passage into an ongoing, potentially eternal material mode of existence, liberated from the illusory ties of species and gravity and unfathomably enriched by absolute connectivity with the ever-expanding potential of undeath. Some people back in my hometown and even in State University think I'm crazy to want to join the OSZ, but I'm entirely committed, of sound mind and body. Anyone who objects can bite me—actually, anyone who supports me can bite me, too, provided they are a Space Zombie!

Mary Marley Latham

Mary is an English Literature Ph.D. candidate at Southern Illinois University of Carbondale. Her essay, "James Bonds of Feminism: Intellectual Antiheroism," is available in the 2016 Crime Uncovered Series collection entitled *Antihero*, and her master thesis, *Apologia Pro Semanalyse: Wordsworth and Kristeva's Maternal Sublime*, is hosted on JEWLScholar. It is then perhaps apparent that Mary is primarily an academic writer. However, since it is her dearest wish that someday someone she does not know will find something she has written, think "this looks interesting," and then read that thing with interest, she is exploring creative writing.

One Million Names for Cinderella
By Nina Moldawsky

12 facts about Big Ben. 20 facts on the London Eye. 10 mentions of the House of Parliament. 120 minutes of lecture on the London Tower.

"Okay, walking-encyclopedia, is there anything you *don't* know?" I asked Ali, my unwanted tour guide, as he lead me to the entrance of the Millennium Bridge past a man blowing three foot bubbles with a net and like, a thousand happy-go-lucky tourists.

"Well sure! There are plenty of things I don't know!" he exclaimed with the wide grin I'd found so charming. Indeed, I'd found that grin charming when he'd leaned over Aunt Susan's garden wall yesterday morning to boldly introduce himself.

I thought that British English and American English were almost the same thing, but apparently a mistranslation happened. See, I said, "I'm your neighbor's house-arrested niece," and he heard, "I'm from America and your country fills me with boundless wonder." Then he said, "I'll show you around the city," which apparently means "I'll give you a laborious, unrelenting history lesson." What a silly American girl I am for not knowing that.

"Uh huh," I nodded dubiously as our shoes clanged on the metal surface of the bridge, "and *what* don't you know?"

"Danny, you can't exactly ask me to tell you things that I *don't* know," he laughed.

That sounds like a challenge.

"Fine," I smirked, "Did you know that… male bees are useless to the hive."

"Other than impregnating queens, yeah, they just mill about don't they?" he grinned smugly, stopping and leaning his arm out on the guardrail.

I popped my hip against the railing and crossed my arms. "Okay. Did you know that...

Redwell, New Mexico is the most boring town on the planet?"

"That's subjective," he chuckled, "but as a matter of fact, you've mentioned your hometown, *and* your hate of it."

"Alright, know-it-all. How about Cinderella? Did you know in the original story, the stepsisters cut off parts of their feet to fit the shoe?" I remembered an *actually* interesting fact.

"That's wrong actually," he shook his head. I grimaced.

"No. It's not."

"You're thinking of the Brothers Grimm version of the fairy tale, that's not the 'original.'"

I softened a bit, out of curiosity. "It's not?"

"It's hard to say who first wrote 'Cinderella' really, because before anything it was an oral story, and those morphed and shifted from person to person. In a way, every storyteller was an author in their own right, they *all* wrote Cinderella. *If* you had to trace it back to an 'original,' as you put, well, we'd have to look far back in history."

I sighed. *Here we go.*

"The version of Cinderella that is closest to the Disney version everyone knows and loves is the 1697 tale of Cendrillon by French author Charles Perrault. The story existed before then, of course, but he wrote in the elements that most *everyone* can pinpoint as essential, like the-the fairy godmother, the changing pumpkin, the glass slippers, the—"

"How did the story exist without the slippers?" I cut in.

"Ali, Ali," I interrupted him, "the point."

"No, it had slippers, but Perrault made them glass! Actually, linguists and historians speculate that 'glass' might've been a mistake, or mistranslation, see—"

"Right. Anyways, Charles Perrault, he added all those recognizable elements, but he adapted the story from a 1634 version, Cenerentola, penned by Giambattista Basile—his version was different, it didn't have Perrault's elements and the prince, uh, I think he was a King instead, which is closer to the Chinese version."

"Chinese version?" I asked.

"Yes! That version is *ancient*, recorded I believe in the ninth century. In that story she was 'Yeh Shen' and the 'godmother' role was replaced by some fish bones," Ali leaned towards me, excited over his prolific facts.

"Fascinating." I nodded.

"But Danny, there's an even *older* recording of the same story, an Egyptian tale in 200 BC! It's amazing, Danny, it's *amazing!*" he insisted, wild eyed.

I don't get it. He's so enthusiastic, packed full of useless trivia and proud of it. If it was one subject, then maybe I'd get it, but no. He's been this way all day, about Big Ben, the London Eye, everything—he knows *everything*, he's excited about *everything*. I could never be that passionate about anything.

I grinned, amused. He's unbelievable.

"Okay. What's your favorite version?" I asked.

"Oh, none of those," he leaned back.

I guffawed. "Are there more?"

"I told you at the beginning, there are *millions*," he answered, continuing before I had the option to protest, "I think if there are so many versions in so many different eras in so many different regions, all of the same story, then there's *got* to be more to it. I think, something must've really happened, something to inject the story into the human conscious. A real princess, maybe. Ah, but in so many times? Hmm, a time traveler, or… an immortal! Cursed to live the same story over and over again through the turns of time."

"Are you serious?"

"Of course," he looked down at me with deadly serious intent.

I nodded slowly, wide eyed. *Okay, dude's crazy.*

I mean, seriously? He thinks there's some magical-ass immortal playing Cinderella dress-up every couple-hundred years? That's ridiculous. *He's* ridiculous, and yet I'm letting him talk my ear off. I shook my head and started snickering.

"God, if 'Cinderella' actually happened, I promise you it went nothing like that." I leaned down on the railing, watching as a ferry tutted through the murky waters of the River Thames.

"How'd it go then? In your mind," he matched my posture, twisting his neck towards me with the eyes of an overexcited puppy.

"Alright. Let's see…" I pressed a thumb to my lips, scheming for something twice as ridiculous to throw back at him. "Ok. I got it."

"Pray tell," he waved me on.

"Ok, so, Cinderella is a bitchy teen who's broken home has taught her love doesn't exist. She cries and whines that her step-mom is 'never gonna understand her' because she makes her do the dishes."

Ali snorted. I chuckled, pleased I'd succeeded in capturing the attention of this serial rambler, and continued.

"So then the King is like, gonna sell off his son to whatever slut is pretty. And Cinderella sees the prince in a magazine—"

"Magazine?"

"Fine, a painting, or a cave drawing, I don't give a fuck. Point is, she sees him, she's like, '*damn, have my babies*,' but her 'awful' step-mom is like, bitch, you're a fucking, *teenager*, you got a life ahead of you, ok? I'm not gonna let you run off and become some rich guy's arm candy. Of course, Cinderella's like 'wah, wah, woe is me,' and prays and prays that God, or Santa, or the Easter Bunny will show up and make her dreams come true, but they don't, because magic doesn't exist."

"Ouch." Ali shook his head.

"So instead she digs up a bunch of cash her dad told her to 'save for something really important' and blows it *all* on like, a dress and stuff. She goes to this party for the guy—prince, whatever, and she's like 'hey, hey, look at my expensive dress, come here often' and he's like, 'yeah, this is my house.'"

Ali laughed.

"But the prince, he starts chatting her up and stuff, and you know, turns out he's actually a pretty chill dude. They end up sneaking up onto the roof, so that the prince's crazy dad will stop trying to introduce him to a bunch of whores. And they just sit on the roof and talk about whatever, you know, stupid facts about the stars and life and their stupid homes and their stupid families."

"A twist!" Ali commented.

"Yeah, I bet you weren't expecting something, well, positive," I laughed.

"I'll be honest, no." He nodded. "But please, finish the story."

I paused a moment, unsure myself where the story was going.

"Well, it's like midnight, parties over, the dad's fuming downstairs wondering where the hell his son is and they're still chilling on the roof. The prince, he says 'hey, so I know my dad's totally crazy, and this whole, finding a queen thing is ridiculous, but I don't know, if it has to happen, I think it'd be a little less crazy and ridiculous with you.'"

Ali touched a hand to his heart.

"And Cinderella… runs. She runs, and runs, and runs… The End."

"What?" Ali balked, "that's it?"

"Not enough?" I grumbled.

"I'd say no."

"Fine. She runs away, crashes her car, and gets sent to live with her aunt in London. Happy?" I blurted.

"Oh." His face paled.

I grimaced, pushed off the railing, brushed past Ali and stuffed my hands into the pockets of my jean shorts.

"Danny!" he called. I sped up. "Wait! I was just gonna say I didn't know that!"

I paused, looking up at him.

He smiled. "That's a thing I didn't know."

I snorted, continuing to walk. "Sure."

He caught up to me and I shook my head, amused. Amused, but, ready to change the subject.

"Okay, 12 facts about Millennium Bridge. Go."

Nina Moldawsky

Nina Moldawsky is a Creative Writing student at Columbia College Chicago. She's had an active writing career since age 14, when she self-published her first novel, and her second a year later.

As a senior in high school she won multiple Scholastic Awards, including a Gold Key for her novel manuscript. More recently her work has been published in her college's online literary magazine, and she writes freelance for a zombie apocalypse live action roleplay game company. Beyond literature and zombies, Nina is also passionate about music and performance arts, and has followed these passions by writing and directing two musicals performed at the Reel Kids theater in Boulder, CO. Someday she hopes to write meaningful stories for children and teens, and until then you can find her perusing coffee shops and gardens, searching for a spark.

Precognition
BY EMILY PORTER

In the far, right corner of the dimly lit room there sits a silver table, illuminated solely by a digital alarm clock blinking the time in red, and the constant flickering of the light emanating from an old rusty lamp. They sit unsteadily upon the shimmering surface of the nightstand, teetering from the blow of the wind that enters by way of the open window. Also on the metallic table top is an open book titled *Decoding Dreams: Revealing the Secrets of Your Unconscious Mind*, the second part to a seemingly never-ending series about understanding the complexity of one's own subconscious. Each page is worn out from foolishly obsessive reading habits. The pages are covered in personal notes, drawn in neat and precise penmanship, while certain sentences and definitions have been highlighted obsessively over six times in a blinding yellow. A pair of old, tattered reading glasses are placed gingerly on the exposed pages, marking the page where he

stopped reading. Next to this corner table sits an old and creaky
wooden bed cloaked in wrinkled, white sheets that are long overdue
for a wash. He lays entangled in the sheets from a night of restless
attempts at sleep - something he has yet to fully conquer in the way
he would like - yet he has managed to fall into a disastrously long
slumber.

A mouse scurries across the floor towards a plate of moldy
food beside the bed, and across the way a colony of ants welcomes
itself into the small apartment where crumbs are scattered in tiny
piles all around. The wood floors are worn out and they creak with
every step he takes during his constant pacing, a habit he cannot
seem to break. Down the hall in the bathroom, the floors are damp
with soiled water from the overflow of the toilet. It finally stopped
running over onto the tile once the plumber came to fix it, but the
damage had already been done. When he asked the man if he would
also clean the mess, the man merely responded by saying, "Not in my
job description," before accepting his payment and quickly exiting
the repugnant apartment. Of course, he had known that it would
break, but no matter how much it bothered him, he refused to clean
the mess by himself until he could understand how it could be that

he knew. These days he always seems to know what is going to occur before morning has even broken.

He's not quite sure when the strange occurrences began. A year ago possibly — has it only been three months? Or maybe it's been a mere few days that have been unreasonably stretched in relation to time, purely in his mind. In truth, none of this sincerely matters. Nothing matters to him as long as the softening sound of his malicious enemy calls to him in the dead of night. Sleep is a burden that causes nothing but fear, and coward is a term he never associated with himself until now. Afraid of sleep? It sounds preposterous, even to him, though he is beginning to understand the consequences that even a light snooze may bring.

It started off simple enough; the first time it occurred, he dreamt that in the office breakroom he would receive two bags of sour cream and onion potato chips instead of the usual single packet during his lunch break. Truly, it's an odd dream to have visualized — realistic to the point that when he awoke for the day, the usual surroundings of his bedroom seemed unfamiliar. Sure enough, two bags fell from the vending machine at lunch, and an unusual sense washed over him, though he figured it was merely a coincidence. But other "coincidences" transpired that day as well, such as Keith McAlister's old, gray stapler crashing to the floor from the shove of his elbow, followed by Keith's huffed, "Darn," and John Atwood accidentally shredding almost an entire box of the wrong files. He recognized every occurrence throughout the day, because he had already seen them in his dreams from the night before. Day after day, he began to predict what was going to happen and when, but he could never comprehend how, and the paranoia eventually destroyed his ability to stay focused at work. Certain things he could stop, like the time he caught Kathy's arm before she hit the floor from tripping on a ripped corner of the carpet, but he couldn't do anything about the time Frank was laid off, and it physically hurt him to sit atop this information throughout the entirety of the day without being able to do a single thing.

When he visualized his own employment being terminated in his sleep, he knew that he couldn't take action this time as well. He had his miniature knick-knacks, personal photos and other belongings from their usual spot on his cubicle desk packed into a small cardboard box before he had even been called into the boss's office. There was no use in fighting back this time, and although he had already heard exactly what Mrs. Brown would say to him once before in the middle of the night, it stung just as much the second time around. "Your sudden incompetence in completing your work up to our company's standards is astounding, Mr. Forrester." Incompetent? Him? He had been working there for nearly ten years, and never once had he heard that word leave her lips in association with his own name. Yet, this is the one time he would not argue with her, for he had been so consumed by his irrational fear of sleep that he could get nothing done besides his tireless contemplation regarding how it could be at all possible.

Eventually, he began to keep a dream journal, which still rests precisely under his pillow at night and candidly in his arms to be carried with any other needed possessions of his during the day. Every morning, immediately after waking up, he hastily grabs the pen from his bedside table and writes, describing in detail every moment of his dream that he can remember, strategically placing them in chronological order.

At his high school reunion, where he knew he would most likely never have to see the people surrounding him again — so long as he didn't show up to the next reunion — he even revealed his journal to a close friend from his past. The concept sounded insane even to himself, so it was no surprise that Kevin Harris, a man he hadn't spoken to in years, called him exactly that before storming off to find his wife. Although Kevin did reconsider, if only for a moment, when he ultimately found her cheating with their old trigonometry teacher in the women's bathroom, something he had warned Kevin about beforehand in his obnoxiously long and seemingly senseless rant.

He left the party that evening questioning his sanity, and the beers he grabbed afterwards at the local underground bar down the street from his apartment building did nothing to ease his restlessness. There was no reasonable explanation, and after passing out drunk on his old, worn couch and waking up the next day only to experience the day's events for a second time, his hope of ever finding reason dwindled far too quickly. All he knew to be true was the events that played out before his eyes every day; every good thing, every great thing and every bad thing, every misstep, every fumble and every falling out. Every day he'd go through the motions, completing odd jobs that would give him just enough money to pay his rent, and every night he tried desperately to stay awake, hoping that whatever type of precognition he had been experiencing would go away with time. Most nights he passed out anyway. Concentration always loses the fight against fatigue.

His feelings about uncovering a way to control this misery in his life only intensified with time, and on his way back from his one o'clock dog walk – one of the jobs he completed every Tuesday and Thursday – he slowed by the steps of the local library just as he had done in his sleep. Research was a last resort as his laziness only grew since he got fired from his first job, but he was desperate. He took a quick look down at his shoe and wished that no one would notice the smell. Rocky, the Pomeranian mutt, crapped on his canvas shoes when he stopped the whole pack for a group water break, but as he recalled from his memory, it was either let Rocky take a dump or let Blue grab the food truck taco right out of a young woman's hands. Putting his own needs behind him, he chose to stop the latter.

Inside the building the ceiling was decorated with speckled white tiles and dreadfully bright overhead lighting. Section W-102 called to him, and he remembered waltzing over to that section in his dream, happening upon a book by a philosopher about something called "lucid dreaming." There, right next to the book that now sits illegally highlighted on his nightstand, was a curious book with black binding and absolutely nothing else on the cover besides the title, *Lucid Dreaming*, and the author's name, Peter Walsh. Never in his life had he owned a library card, but that changed very quickly in one afternoon. Back at his apartment, which at the time was undergoing the process of turning into the pigsty it is today, he opened the book so hastily that the first page actually tore at the edge. It didn't matter, but the words on the pages definitely did. Lucid dreaming was a peculiar method of sleeping, one that allowed the dreamer to control every single aspect of what occurred in their unconscious world. It was the solution to his problems that he had been desperately looking for, but little did he know that the consequences would be so immense.

Immediately he began to train himself in order to conquer this new theoretical solution, following the process that old Walsh listed for the reader at the very end. He knew that he had to learn this skill quicker than he had ever learned anything in his life. In fact, as the growing sense of desperation and extreme fatigue finally settled in, it became his only hope. He could no longer afford to continue the unhealthy routine of forcibly remaining awake through the night, so he immersed himself in Walsh's teachings.

His first attempts were unsuccessful, as expected, but to consciously dream is a difficult process for someone who has lived their life in a state of ceaseless worrying and anxiety for innumerous days. The step by step guide explained that it would take time to become fully aware and in control of his dreams, and even longer to become accustomed to the feeling of consciousness without the ability to physically move. The brain is hard at work, allowing one to regulate the outcome of his or her dream, and all the while the body sleeps through the night, immovable until the person 'lucid dreaming' finally awakes. It is a strange feeling, and something that sometimes only causes discomfort and anxiety in those who try, as it becomes difficult to differentiate the reality and the subconscious. But there are tricks, such as counting the fingers on one's hand or reading the time on a clock. In dreams, hands have more fingers or sometimes fewer, and clocks read impossible times that would make absolutely no sense in the real world. This all made him uncomfortable with the thought of even attempting this strange and new process, but without any other options to help him there was nothing left for him to do. That is, unless he wanted to continue out the rest of his days as he had been.

Without time on his side, he had no other option than to fully dedicate his days and nights to overcoming all obstacles in his path, ultimately leading to his gaining the ability to knowingly dream. The first time he was successful, after practically perfecting his pre-sleep ritual and technique, the day played out in his favor. It wasn't anything too suspicious or impractical. On that Monday he would find a twenty-dollar bill in his pants pocket that he couldn't remember putting there, and the person in front of him in line at the dinky, cheap, corner café on his street would offer to pay for his coffee. Nothing malicious, only simple things meant to brighten his own day, and when all of this actually happened, he had blurred the line between dream and reality.

With continuous practice, he found that he could control the outcomes of the lives of others throughout the day as well, making other's lives as easy as his own. On the upcoming Friday, when the Wall-Street-type banker passed the homeless man who lived outside the building on his way to work, he would uncharacteristically take $100 out of his wallet to place in the donation cup of the disheveled, sleeping man. He only once used his newfound command of the day's fate to negatively mess with his neighbor, where her window was unknowingly left open at night and she awoke to twenty birds comfortably living inside her home. In his own defense, she was the angriest, meanest woman he had ever had the displeasure of meeting, and he felt that this was justifiable.

Eventually he tried to change fate on a larger scale, in an entirely different country, but whenever he tried to move past the edge of his neighboring burrow, something pulled him back, almost as if an invisible boundary was placed strategically around him, allowing him to only control within a few miles' radius. But he was a goodhearted man, despite the cruel trick on his apartment neighbor, and he tried countless times to escape these boundaries, though each attempt was deemed a failure. As the days moved forward, he learned to fully comprehend this newfound power. He now knew that everyone's lives were in his hands, and he could change whatever he wanted, so long as it was within the distance set by whatever strange force gave him this power in the first place.

On a particularly good day, where the lives of every single foster child in the building two streets away changed for the better when loving families came to adopt every last one, he prepared himself for sleep at night and disregarded his usual routine, assuming he could finally lucid dream without it. The next day was disastrous. Half of the children had been returned, but there was nowhere for them to go when their home, full of all of their memories, became engulfed in flames and burnt to the ground. The story was on the local and national news, and newspapers and magazines wrote harrowing articles about the incident, stating that it would take over a year to fix all of the damage. One shouldn't play with fate for the same reason that one would never change the events of history, there's always the possibility that the outcome might be disastrous. That day he dealt with a guilt like no other, and it weighed him down in a way that felt as though something was pulling him through the worn fabric of his lumpy mattress. He never skipped his pre-dreaming routine again.

There are times though, despite his mastery over the authority of his dreaming, that no matter how hard he tries to gain jurisdiction at night, sleep only leads him into an uncontrollable stream of unconsciousness, hence his exhausted form lying fast asleep cradled in his sheets. He mistakenly skipped a step in his ritual, and now he had catastrophic consequences to face.

The mouse drags a crumbled piece of the stale bread underneath the frame of the bed, and the ants travel between piles of morsels as the first light of day peeks through the window. Loud shouting and stomping feet from the apartment above startle him awake. He angrily snaps his head to face the source of the noise. This is for the best based on the dark shift of direction that his dream had taken, it's better for everyone that he arises early this morning. Too much damage had already been done. He mutters incoherently to himself, obviously irritable about taking a step back in the training of his mind and reaches underneath his pillow to pull out the bright red leather journal. Furiously, he flips to a new page with one hand and grabs the black ballpoint pen from the bedside table with the other, uncapping it to scribble in the date on the top right corner of a fresh page. There's only so much time left for him to write everything down, but without this journal, everything he could remember envisioning would be lost.

Throwing back the top sheet and swinging his legs around to the edge of the bed, he stands and runs over to the closet, silently cursing as he grabs a pair of ripped jeans that he has had since college and a gray sweatshirt, littered with holes. After getting down on all fours to peer under the bed, he finds his wallet at the very edge, hoping something inside of it will help him try and stop the events of today. He empties its contents on to the floor; there are two $10 bills and $0.87 in change, as well as an expired Visa gift card that has lived in the leather pouch for over six years. He clutches it and buries it inside of his left-hand pocket, although he knows it will most likely be of no use to him. Outside of the bedroom, he slips on his sneakers, still covered in Rocky's gift from that past afternoon and tied with mismatched laces. He stashes his journal under his arm before snatching the key beside the door and running out of his apartment.

If only I hadn't screwed it up, he thinks to himself on the way out, going through what it was that he missed in his little bedtime ceremony. The elevator is broken, and it has been since he moved here. Of course, he has the power to change that, but his nasty neighbor complains about it so much that he's willing to take the stairs just so she has to suffer through them as well. He races down the steps, accidentally knocking the groceries out of his neighbor's arms in the process. She curses at him as he flies out of the entryway, and he's frustrated with her constant need to yell at him, but he knows that she is the least of his worries at this point.

Stopping on the corner he pulls his notebook out from under his arm, attempting to piece together the future events of today in his head. He's just about to move on to the Antique Boutique across the street, the place where the first event of his dream, a robbery, takes place, but he hears multiple people shouting from behind. Everyone is yelling at each other to move out of the way, and all of a sudden he knows exactly what time of day it is. Turning around, hoping that he will be wrong and that it is not already too late, he is immediately disappointed. A large, eighteen-wheeler is barreling through the streets, the driver honking frantically, the brakes obviously broken and useless, as a man sits in his car at the stoplight fervently trying to

escape before his fate is decided for him, but the locks on the doors

are jammed. *If only.*

Emily Porter

Emily Porter is 21 years-old and a student at Hofstra University where she is studying English with a concentration in publishing studies and literature, and minoring in marketing. After graduation, Emily plans to pursue a career in publicity and marketing within the world of publishing. She also hopes to one day run a bi-annual literary magazine brimming with personal narratives to be used as a tool in spreading intelligence and information about the issues regarding social justice. Emily lives with her mom, dad, brother, sister, cat, and two dogs, Hettie and Ginger, who are both the light of her life. If she isn't writing a story or reading a great book, you can probably find her pulling an all-nighter in the library to write an essay. This is Emily's first time being published.

From the Window of a Heart Hospital in Clovis

By Sierra Saykeo

There's something about a missed call in the middle of the day that is especially ominous to me.

My cousin rarely ever called. We grew up together, played together as children. But we were older now. We had our own lives, our own responsibilities, our own scraped knees to deal with. I was headed into an orthodontist appointment when I noticed that he had called. I had a few minutes to spare, so I called him back.

"Hey, did you mean to call?"

"You need to come to California."

He said this often, and I thought nothing of it at first. I always needed to go, he said, because most of my family lived there. My dad, he missed me. Life was better there apparently, more fun. But this time was different. The details of the call are lost on me now. But I hung up knowing that this time, I really did need to go to California.

The small detail of still going into my appointment after having just received a call about my dad being in the hospital is so remarkable to me now. It didn't occur to me then—the harsh reality of still wanting to carry out my mundane obligations so as to not cause any inconvenience to others when, in all honesty, I was having a hard time keeping it together. I was faced with the very real threat of my father passing at any moment, and I knew that as his only child, it was my sole responsibility to care for him. But all that seemed to matter in the moment was that my bottom row of teeth were crowding.

I was scheduled to get my teeth sandpapered that day. As the lady violently tugged and jerked the piece of sandpaper around and against my bottom incisors, she lectured me about my gums bleeding, and the importance of flossing. My thoughts kept wandering back to my dad—how was he? How long had he been sick? Was I going to be able to handle whatever waited for me in California?

I had trouble fighting the oncoming tears.
"Oh I'm sorry, honey. I know it hurts."

***

I flew to California the very next morning. I watched Christmas and New Years pass from the window of a heart hospital in Clovis that also happened to have a good view of the Sierra mountain range—which I was named after. My dad was very resistant to being taken care of at times, and I couldn't help but be angered by this. Despite my constant begging, he would sometimes refuse to eat.

When the nurses started lecturing him about how he needed to eat to get better, he made me eat his meals in secret so that it would appear as though he was.

There wasn't much to separate my experience from any other typical hospital experience: the sleeping in uncomfortable positions in chairs, the incessant beeping of unfamiliar machines, the nauseating disinfectant smell, the being woken up every hour by nurses checking vitals. I was strung along by different doctors who often responded to my urgency with alarming apathy.

"We'll know when the blood cultures come back in the morning," they'd say. But each morning brought a new problem, another delay in getting the answers we needed. My skin broke out because of the constant stress, and I began to feel that I had no anchor in the real world. There were a couple of defining moments where I truly felt that I had lost my mind:

Like when I started to get emails about the syllabi for my upcoming Spring semester classes and I ran to one of the waiting rooms to keep from having a panic attack in front of my dad—two worlds of responsibility colliding;

Or the time I spoke for my father, who had a hard time articulating himself in English, and the doctor interrogated me about whether I was *really* his daughter, or just a close family friend. "Biological or adopted," she had to inquire further?;

And once a lady woke me out of my sleep to ask questions about insurance. "Ma'am?" She said, tapping my shoulder. Once I was fully awake I broke into tears. I was not old enough for anyone to call me "ma'am." I was not old enough to answer questions about insurance policies. I was not old enough to potentially plan a funeral.

I was usually too afraid to leave my dad alone in the room. I asked my cousin to bring an empty notebook to the hospital during one of her visits so I could try to write. However, every time I went to put pen to paper, I would either be too tired, too uninspired, or be interrupted by nurses or my dad needing something. I ended up spending most of my time playing virtual pool on my phone, trying to read people's lips on the muted hospital television or just staring out of the window at the mountains.

I found only one daily reprieve from all of the madness. Fearing that I'd miss the doctors when they made their morning rounds, I began to write down the times they typically visited the room. There was a sweet spot at around 7:00 AM when the nurses would be switching shifts, before the cardiologist, nutritionist, or other doctors came, and right after my dad fell asleep, typically tired out from a whole night of pain and restlessness. When 7 AM hit, I would slip out and sneak off to the hospital's cafeteria for just a moment. I'd trot over to the refrigerated goods and pluck out a carton of vanilla soy milk. The carton was charming—small, purple, and shaped like a kid's juice box. I'd also pick up a plastic cup full of fruit for my dad, which he never ate. I'd make my way quickly over to the cashier station, pay, and slip silently back into the room. The whole ordeal only took a matter of minutes, but it became one of the only times I'd leave the room and one of the only predictable things about my days in the hospital.

I'd set the cup of fruit on my dad's tray and sit, excited to drink my soy milk. I felt like a kid again—unwrapping the straw, puncturing the top, holding the compact box in both hands, sipping quietly. It felt wrong to enjoy something, especially something so trivial. I had an impressive collection of cartons lining the windowsill until one day, I had gone to my cousin's just to shower and gather new clothes and found that a nurse had thrown them all away.

***

My relationship with my father has always been strange, strained, or complicated or, more likely, some combination of the three. I'm hesitant to admit that I was embarrassed by him during my younger years. When he managed to make it to my elementary school functions, I couldn't escape the taunting of other kids. They'd ask questions like, *Why is his skin so much darker than yours? Why does he talk like that?* At lunch once, a friend of mine leaned into me, cupping her sticky hands around my ear and whispered, *Are you sure that's really your dad?*

I stopped asking him to come to my school.

Karma appeared to come back full circle though, as it seemed I spent every moment afterwards trying to prove that I *was* his daughter.

I remember one particular Lao New Year, my dad had taken me to the temple. He usually kept me close to his side rather than letting me play with the hordes of children running around, chasing each other with water guns and shaving cream. As a result, I just sat around bored, eating, and listening to my dad's conversations with other adults. I became used to other members of the community coming up to talk to him and eventually turning their attention to me. Being the only obviously mixed child at these events made me a topic of conversation. I felt like a fish in an aquarium, surrounded by people poking the glass. Bored of their bewilderment, I'd bow my head and let them talk about me like I wasn't there. They'd ask my dad how I was so light, if I knew Thai or Lao and when had he had a kid with a white woman?

Two women approached my dad, already eyeing me. As they greeted him, I dropped my food to greet them in return. I put my hands together, fingertip-to-fingertip. I lowered my head and brought my hands up so that the tips of my pointer fingers graced the tip of my nose. Determined to prove myself, I murmured a greeting in Thai. *Sawatdee krahp.*

The women snickered, seemingly amused. It wasn't until the women walked away that my dad turned to me and said, "Sawatdee krahp is for men. You need to say 'Sawatdee kah.'"

Something in his voice felt like admonishment, like he was ashamed. The embarrassment caused an immediate heat to rise in the back of my neck, reaching the tips of my ears. I was mortified. I was so aware of my otherness it made my skin crawl.

***

My dad's diagnosis eventually came. It turned out that he somehow had contracted pneumonia that then spread to one of the valves in his heart, which needed to be replaced. The surgery and his recovery brought its own, unique cases of hopelessness, and anxiety. The hospital staff sent me home for two days while my dad underwent the surgery and recovered for a day in ICU. When they called me and told me I could come back and the surgery was successful, I rushed to the hospital, thinking the hardest part was over. The ICU room was bleak to say the least. Besides the usual hospital equipment, the walls were blank; there was no television, just two chairs and a small window at the far side of the room. I walked in to see my dad in a chair next to his hospital bed. He was hunched over, holding a stuffed animal, a moose, tightly against his chest. His nurse later told me that it was to relieve any of the pressure in his chest while breathing or mobile. He looked like a child in pain. Most likely out of embarrassment, he averted his eyes away from my gaze. But by this small gesture that, for some reason, felt like rejection, I sunk into the chair by the window, hung my head in my hands, and silently cried.

Amidst all of the chaos and uncertainty, one moment stands out on its own among the rest, a moment that continues to move me:

Before we got his official diagnosis, there was a time in the middle of the night when my dad called out to me. Thinking something was wrong; I panicked and rushed to get up, almost tripping over myself. I stepped to the side of his bed, cringing at the contact between my bare feet and the cold, hard hospital floor.

"I want to eat. Will you feed me that fruit?" he pointed with his head in the direction of the tray that the nurses had brought him earlier that day.

I picked up the small cup of fruit and the fork and picked out pieces of cantaloupe, melon, and pineapple—his favorites. I could hear his teeth squeaking as he chewed. In between bites, I couldn't help but look at his face. He seemed to have gotten so much older just in the past month. He was tired, I could tell. His features were much harder, sharper, perhaps because of all the weight he lost. I wanted to cry at how frail he really looked, but I knew that I couldn't, or I'd risk upsetting him. I had to resist the urge to wonder if this was an act of giving up.

I was moved, still, by the tenderness of the moment. Through all of the talking with doctors, nurses, insurance ladies; through all of the taking him on short walks around the halls of the hospital, helping him use the bathroom, and adjusting blankets in the middle of the night when he got too hot or too cold; this was the first time that I felt I was really helping him.

My dad has often said, and still says to this day, that I am the only thing he has left anymore. I admit that this has always sounded a little overstated to me, considering he lives in California with nearly all of his side of the family. Only then though, in that moment, was I getting the sense that he really might mean it.

I pushed the thought away and continued to feed him.

Sierra Saykeo

Sierra Saykeo was born in Redding, California, but raised in Greensboro, North Carolina. Even though she is a Psychology major and spends most of her time writing research papers, poetry and short stories remain as some of her greatest passions. You can find

Sierra either playing with her newly adopted kitten, Kylo, eating an overabundance of Asian food, playing video games, or drinking cheap white wine while watching strange documentaries. She is currently working on a bucket list that includes: getting published, seeing BTS live in concert, and taking a cross-country trip by train. One down, plenty more to go.

Death Comes For All Things
By Fiona Shampine

The death of Baldr was one of my most trying experiences as the goddess of death. He is the son of Odin after all and he's beloved by everyone and everything. No one wanted him to stay dead. Such is the way of the world though, I suppose. No one wants to accept death. You cry, you rail, but you can never defeat death. Death is inevitable. But that's beside the point. You want to hear the story of the death of the golden boy of the Asgardians. Everything began one day when I was visited by Huginn and Muninn. The conversation proceeded as many conversations with Odin did.

"Hel Lokidottir, Queen of Niflheim, Mother of the dishonorable dead." Odin's voice boomed out of the beaks of the ravens. "I wish to speak to you."

"Odin," I said, keeping my voice calm and level. "What brings you here?" I was in the middle of updating my ledger at the moment. I keep a book with all the names of my wards in it. I have their life stories written down in those pages so that no one is ever truly forgotten.

"My son and wife have been having dreams of your kingdom," Odin said. "They dream of death and my son's destruction. Are you behind this?" I resisted the urge to roll my eyes.. How my father had become blood brothers with this man was beyond me.

"No, uncle, I am not," I replied. "Besides, your wife made everything in existence swear an oath not to harm Baldr, did she not? Now, I would very much like to finish my work if you don't mind."

"That is all you have to say on the matter?" Odin sounded almost surprised that I would dare to be so flippant towards him.

"Yes, that is all I have to say on the matter," I said. "I'm not my father. I don't cause trouble needlessly." The birds glanced at one another. It seemed they weren't satisfied with my response.

"Should he die, you will be held responsible."

"I can make no exceptions. If he dies, then he shall be welcomed into my kingdom with open arms," I said. Why would I be held responsible, anyway? There was only one thing on Earth that hadn't sworn an oath and I hadn't been involved in that. It wasn't my fault that mistletoe hadn't sworn to never harm Baldr.

"He is my son! He cannot be allowed to die!" Odin roared. I stood my ground, staring intently at my uncle's ravens.

"Death is a natural part of life," I reminded him. "Everyone dies."

"Not us!" Odin insisted. "Not the gods!"

"So, you think you deserve special treatment?" I could feel anger bubbling up despite my attempts to suppress it. "You think that just because you're the king of the gods you get to break all the rules you want?"

"That's not what I'm saying-"

"Yes, it is," I said. "And this is one rule I will not let you break. Death comes for all things. Even the gods." For a long time, we simply stared at one another. Once it was clear I wasn't about to back down, Odin finally yielded.

"Very well." I could hear him gritting his teeth. "But this conversation is not over. We will speak again." Then his little spies flew away. I stood there for a few minutes, taking deep shaking breaths until I was finally calm again. Something about the Asgardians always brought out the worst in me. They frustrated me to no end. They could break all the rules they wanted, while my family was punished just for existing. I truly was the villain in every story of theirs. Nothing I did was right. I sat back down, trying to force myself to work again. Unfortunately for my work, I didn't get too far before my father appeared.

"I saw the soot sprites were here," he said, poking his head into my study. "What did they want?"

"Baldr's been having dreams of me." I said. "Of my kingdom. I suspect he'll be coming here." I also suspected my father would be responsible for Baldr's death. Why else would Odin have sent his ravens if he didn't think the same thing?

"You know, most women would rip you apart for the chance to live with Baldr," my father laughed.

"He's my cousin." I wrinkled my nose. "And have you forgotten he's married?"

"How could I forget?" My father flopped down onto a chair in the corner of my study. "All he ever does is talk about his wife nowadays. Nanna this and Nanna that."

"You would do well to follow in his footsteps," I whispered. The way he treated my stepmother was horrid. She deserved so much better.

"What was that, pumpkin?" My father asked, looking over.

"Nothing," I said quickly.

"Alright." My father shrugged. "So, how'd the whole talk with the old man go?" He had a nervous gleam in his eye that seldom meant good things.

"About as well as it usually does." I pursed my lips, putting the ledger back on my desk. I was lucky it hadn't gotten any worse. My father whistled.

"Baldr's really gonna die, huh?" He said. "Geez, didn't think it could happen."

"Death comes for all things. Even the gods," I repeated. I had to believe that. This was one rule that could not be broken, no matter how hard Odin tried. Part of me did feel bad that Baldr would be caught up in this war between my family and the Asgardians. He didn't deserve death. But then again, no one did.

"So, how's he going to die? He doesn't do anything dangerous."

"I don't know." I sat down across from him, searching his features for any sign of scheming. My father was looking right past me, eyes narrowed slightly. He was formulating some kind of revenge plan again. My heart sank. I didn't need this. Not now.

"Father, whatever you're thinking of doing, please don't," I begged. "He doesn't deserve this. He may be the son of Odin, but he shouldn't suffer for the sins of his father. Don't stoop to Odin's level." My brothers and I had suffered for years because of my father's actions, causing us to grow angry and bitter. I had been cast down into Niflheim, Jormungandr had been confined to the ocean, and Fenrir had been chained to a rock. We have been deeply hurt. I didn't want Baldr to suffer from the same bitterness that had invaded my heart and soul.

"No promises, pumpkin." My father gave me a lopsided smile and kissed my forehead. "Someone has to pay."

"Father, please." I grabbed his hand as he tried to walk away. "This needs to stop. One of these days you're going to go too far."

"I won't go too far, sweetheart," he assured me. "Everything's going to be fine." A moment later, he was gone, leaving me holding nothing but air. I stared down at my hand, then let it drop.

"Ganglot, Ganglati. Prepare the guest room. We shall have a new addition to the household soon."

——

Balder was rather surprised when he passed through my doors. I suppose it had something to do with the fact that he'd never been to my domain before, and likely never expected to see it. Idunn's apples were powerful things indeed. He was as beautiful as I remembered him being. He was tall but slim, dressed all in white. His golden hair cascaded down his back, so fair it was almost white. His eyes were bluer than the sky, which I hadn't seen in a long time.

"Where am I?" He asked. I rose from my place at the large dinner table and walked over.

"You're in Niflheim. In my kingdom," I said. "I am Hel. Do you remember me?" His face paled at my name. Did he really not remember me? We'd played together as children. We'd been friends once. It hurt to see him looking at me with such fear.

"I do," he said slowly. I could see recognition dawning in his eyes, and shame.

"I'm glad. Would you like me to show you your quarters?" I asked. "You could stay in my hall or with the others in my kingdom. I'm sure the women would be most pleased to see you."

"You're too kind," Balder said, smiling nervously. "That would be nice, thank you." So, I took him to the room I'd prepared.

"I must apologize for the impersonal nature of the room," I said as I opened the door. "I didn't know what you liked."

"That's alright," Baldr assured me, stepping inside. "I...I suppose I'll have a lot of time to decorate it to my tastes." I nodded, watching as he sat down on the bed. His shoulders were beginning to shake.

"Are you alright?" I asked.

"I'm okay." He tried to smile, but he looked to be quickly falling to pieces. I walked over to sit beside him, letting him lean on my shoulder. He began to cry. His tears glowed, like sunshine in liquid form.

"It's alright," I whispered, stroking his hair.

"I j-just...my family," he sobbed into my shoulder. "I'm never going to see them ever again. I won't see my wife ever again."

"You'll see Nanna again," I assured him. "She'll be here soon." All things considering, that wasn't a good thing, but I knew it would make Baldr happy.

"She's...She's coming here?" His eyes widened and he abruptly looked up. "H-How? Why?"

"She throws herself onto your funeral pyre," I said. "She misses you as much as you miss her."

"No no no." He ran his hands through his hair, tears streaming down his cheeks. "She deserves to live! She deserves to have a life!"

"Death happens." I touched his hand, rubbing my thumb across his hand. "It's not fair and it doesn't make sense, but it happens." I squeezed his hand and smiled in what I hoped was a reassuring way. "I want you to be happy here, Baldr."

"You do?" Baldr looked rather like a confused puppy at that moment. It was rather adorable, I have to admit.

"I want all my wards to be happy here," I said. Baldr stared at me for a moment, puzzled, then started laughing.

"What's so funny?" I frowned and let go of his hand.

"You're nothing like everyone says you are," he said with a warm smile.

"Well, you shouldn't believe everything Odin says." I smoothed my dress out self-consciously. "Now, would you like to meet everyone?"

"I'd love that."

———

Things weren't perfect after that. Baldr was happy when Nanna arrived, but the two of them still lamented their deaths. I did what I could to make them feel better, but there was only so much I could do on the matter. That was something they needed to work through on their own. I wasn't surprised by the time Hermod arrived.

I had known Odin would send someone since he didn't want to set foot in my kingdom on his own. Hermod was a rather disgruntled young man who did not look like he wanted to be here at all. I didn't blame him.

"Why have you come here?" I asked, standing in the doorway to my hall as Hermod approached on horseback.

"My father sent me to get my brother back," he replied.

"I can't do that."

"Surely you can do something." He dismounted a pleading look in his eyes. "You're the goddess of death."

"Death is final, cousin."

"Please, he's my brother," Hermod begged. He didn't dare come any closer than the bottom of the stairs, sinking to his knees and clasping his hands in front of him. I knew what I had to do, but it didn't hurt any less. I'd had people come to me before, begging for the return of their loved ones. I suppose that was one reason I have such a dismal reputation. I don't compromise. No one can come back from the dead. There are rules in this world and it is my job to uphold those rules. I can make no exceptions. Not for anyone.

"I can't give him back to you. I'm sorry," I said, letting my cold façade break for a moment.

"Then why can't you give him back?" Hermod demanded. "If you're sorry then why can't you give me my brother back?"

"There are rules."

"But we are gods!"

He wasn't trying to be difficult. He was a young man grieving for his brother. But his attitude was exactly why I couldn't let him take Baldr back to Asgard.

"Death is not a rule that can be broken." I steeled myself, shutting down my emotions. If they wanted to paint me as the villain of their story, then so be it. But I would not let them destroy the order of the world for their own desires.

"I heard yelling, is everything alright?" Baldr stuck his head through the doorway, Nanna at his side.

"Everything is fine," I said. "Please, go back inside."

"Baldr!" Hermod sprung to his feet. "Don't worry, I'm here to take you home! You won't have to suffer in this place any longer!"

"I'm not suffering," Baldr said. "You don't need to worry, brother. I'm fine. Everyone's been so kind to me."

"Hel has been nothing but welcoming," Nanna added. "We've come to terms with our deaths, Hermod. You don't need to worry."

"You...You witch!" Hermod shook his head and pointed accusingly at me. "You've bewitched them, haven't you?"

"I have done no such thing" I snapped. How dare he! I would never harm anyone under my care. My wards are like my own children. I care about them more than I care about myself.

"Hel, it's alright." Baldr gently touched my shoulder. "He's just scared and angry."

"Why aren't you afraid of her?" Hermod demanded. "She's a monster! You've seen her lower half, haven't you?" I unconsciously hunched my shoulders at the mention of my rotten lower half.

"Hermod, that's very rude," Nanna scolded him. "She's self-conscious about that."

"She's captured you!" Hermod was beginning to get worked up. "Can't you see? She's stolen your souls!"

"Hermod, she's just doing her job." Baldr looked towards his brother, shaking his head in disappointment. "You shouldn't be so cruel to her."

"Can't you see that she's manipulating you?" Hermod gestured wildly around. "She's the daughter of the Liesmith!" At this point, I just wanted Hermod to go away. I wanted to go back to my wards, to the people who wouldn't call me cruel names.

"If you want Baldr back, then everything on Earth has to cry for him," I said, folding my arms. "Go report that to your father." Hermod stopped his tirade, his mouth hanging open in shock. Baldr and Nanna were similarly shocked into silence by my proclamation.

"What are you waiting for?" I raised an eyebrow. "I might take the offer back if you don't hurry."

"T-Thank you, my lady!" Hermod nodded and scrambled back to his horse, remounting and riding quickly away.

"Why did you do that?" Baldr asked. "I thought you didn't want to break the rules."

"I had to give him something or he was never going to leave." I turned and headed back towards the dining table.

"But what if they manage it?" Nanna asked. If Baldr was returned to life, she would likely be left behind with me. Odin only cared about his darling son, after all.

"They won't. I know at least one person who won't cry."

———

Predictably, it didn't work. My cousin's murderer did not cry for Baldr. That was when Odin and the other Aesir discovered it had been my father who had murdered Baldr. Originally, they'd assumed it was Hodr, Baldr's brother. Hodr had thrown the mistletoe dart that had pierced Baldr's heart, his hand guided by my father. I don't know what went through my father's mind when he did this. I never do. But nevertheless, I took care of Baldr, Nanna, and even Hodr when he arrived. Death comes for all things. That is the universal truth of the world. But no matter what, if you come to me, you will not be alone. I am always with you. Now and forever.

Fiona Shampine

Fiona was born and raised in Skokie, a suburb of Chicago. She is currently attending Columbia College Chicago to study

Creative Writing with a focus on Fiction. She's been writing for as long as she can remember and can't imagine her life without it. She loves cats, Norse mythology, and fantasy. This is her first publication and she's very excited to share her work with everyone.

Fire and Ice
By Nia Tipton

AMAN SINGH WAS MADE OF GOLD.

The nurse said he was an angel, with 10 little toes and 10 little fingers. He was a beautiful baby boy skin a golden mixture of heritage and pride. His ancestors were strewn on battlefields and brought up in a world of death and enslavement; crimson blood spilling onto earthy battlefields for him to be raised in a world of white. The shackles of before are removed from his name as the nurse wipes him down and wraps him up in a white blanket, cloaking him in what is right before handing him to his mother. Her weary brown eyes wash over his caramel skin, his button nose and closed lips with adoration. She brushes her lips against the skin of his forehead when his father arrives.

His father is a man of his word. He is a man of 6 foot 3 who bears the beatings of prejudice and racism with his head held high and his turban held higher. His beard is combed and neatly set as he strides in, his footsteps commanding and strong for someone who works three jobs to support his family. He settles into his wife's side, the nurses clearing out as the couple look down at the young boy. As the door clicks shut, silence coats them as they take in the miracle before them.

His father raises Aman's tiny fist in his own, brushing the fingers that will write their way to a higher class of life. Pulling it out of his pocket, he slips the Kara onto his wrist, pressing a kiss to the blood that rushes under the skin beneath the circular steel band of metal. Raising his gaze to his wife, he takes in the tiredness and the fear.

The fear of another soul that must bear the brunt of the words of the ignorant; one who must face the world with its white washed masses and its God-fearing leaders.

And so she whispers into the cool British air,

"Ik Onkar."

Not the word printed onto the notes that run the world.

Not the one that commands the country and their every move.

There is only one God, the one who is above and loves unconditionally, no matter what creed, cast or religion.

AMAN SINGH WAS MADE OF QUESTIONS.

He pants as he hides behind the school. His back meets the bricked wall and the grooves dig into his spine but he doesn't bother to move. He has ran long enough from his past and future to bother about his well-being in the present.

He feels sick as he sees his rumaal in tatters in his hands. His mother warned him as she tied the cloth over his head, covering his braided long locks with the fabric of his religion. She told him of the boy's with knives for words; that they would dig a groove into his faith, trying to dislodge it from the firm place within his heart. She told him, 'Ik Onkar, and he will protect you', that God could heal the wounds of the bravest soldiers and that Aman was the bravest of them all. Aman was a fighter and his battle was everyday; breathing and living his eternal war with his golden skin and covered hair.

But she didn't tell him of the hands that would grab and pull, that would rip and tear at the fabric on his head. How they would jeer and taunt him for his 'girl' length hair; for his strange head attire and jewelry that adorned his right wrist.

They weren't taught from their fathers about the everlasting love the steel band signified, or how the cloth on his head was worn by his ancestors who fought for everything that his family believed in. For the air he breathes and the food he eats. They were taught of those who are great and those who are different, fear instilled into their hearts from the day they were born, just like Aman.

With his back pressed against the brick wall and his pride in tatters in his hands he doesn't know anything anymore.

When he gets home, he stays silent as his mother curses the boys who harmed him. He doesn't understand why she would say such words when she stays up late tailoring their mother's country club clothes, her fingers calloused from the pricks of the needle.

He doesn't know why his father seethes silently at the table when he presents his ripped rumaal. He doesn't understand why he would leave the table and lock himself in his study, his mother tongue igniting the air as he shouts at them. Because he knows that on parent's evening they will all whisper about his strong Eastern accent, laughing at the way he lingers on his 'R' and skipping over the 'V'.

He doesn't know anything as he stands in front of his bathroom mirror. His eyes meet the ones in the reflection, full of eight years of fire. He only knows that in this world, to stay alive he must appease the others. So he lifts the scissors he stole from the drawer and raises it to his hair.

And when the first lock falls to the floor and the others soon follow, he doesn't know if there is only one God.

Of if there is a God at all.

AMAN SINGH WAS MADE OF BEAUTY.

The girls flocked around him; sinking their claws into his tanned arms, smearing their fake tan on his caramel complexion. The boys envied him; with his broad shoulders and lean figure, he cut a sharp figure as he raced down the field, skin glowing under the heat as he tucked the ball into his side, thick muscles straining with tension. He ditches three letters for the ease of others, his new identity represented by an 'A', the beginning of his new life.

"Ugh, A, I wish I had hair as thick as yours. It's gorgeous!" Natalie mutters, her fingers combing through his shoulder length hair. It's longer now, grown out to a state that's longer than others but not too long to be strange. Because being different is the worst fate in this God-forsaken world. His head lies in the girl's lap, her long fingers playing with the hair. He rolls his eyes at the comment, setting the book down that he was reading. He chooses to close his eyes, the gentle stroking and massaging of his head reminding him of when he was younger. It reminds him of the way his mother would set him before her, oil in one hand and a fine-toothed comb in the other.

A smile teases his lips as he remembers, Natalie's actions causing him to relax further into her lap. She moves her hand from his head to his face, the aqua on the back of her nail standing out against her pale skin, she presses her rose stained lips to his. Her actions cause him to allow his eyelids to flutter open, to which he sees a halo of blonde framing her heart-shaped pale face. He lifts off of her, cupping her jaw and stroking her cheek tenderly.

"I can't come round tonight," he says, watching carefully as her lips begin to turn down at the edges, "family arrangement."

She sighs heavily, moving out of his grasp, "why don't you invite me to…..-"

"Natalie…" he says, wrapping a hand around her wrist and pulling her back towards him.

"I know, you can't. I just wish that we could… ugh your family is so backwards!" She cries out and he tenses around her.

"Shit, I'm sorry. A, I'm sorry." She apologizes, hands going to his neck to pull him back and closer. Their foreheads press against each other and she lifts up onto her tiptoes to kiss him.

Soft lips slide against the chapped edges of his, the warmth of her tongue poking out to slip into his mouth. He breathes her in, the warmth she provides making him respond to her actions. There are no butterflies; no fireworks igniting in the pit of his stomach. Instead he is content with the situation and the girl in his arms. Her arms slide down his front, playing with his belt as she presses closer to him.

He pulls away, chest heaving with ragged breath. Emotionally and physically he is far from her as he steps away, his hand drags through his hair and he pulls on the ends before turning away, his words carried away by the wind.

"I have to go," he mutters, and then leaves without a goodbye.

AMAN SINGH WAS MADE OF FIRE.

His hand cracks down on his desk, his head shaking as he opens his mouth.

"Segregation isn't the way to move forward, it's moving backwards at least a century." He cries out loud, now rising to his feet. The lecture hall seems dwarfed by his stature, his tweed jacket and tortoise shelled glasses age him further than his 25 years.

"Well, obviously something must be done for our own safety, otherwise they are free to kill civilians." The boy opposite him scoffs. Aman feels his lip curl into a sneer, fists clenching by his side. He is about to respond when someone else cuts in.

"It's perception; you perceive the situation to be one of aggression, that they are against you. They believe it is one of oppression. The root of the problem isn't nuclear warfare concentrated on a place that holds more innocent civilians than criminals. The root of the problem is our own society."

The class ends and Aman finds himself approaching the voice. The man wears a black denim jacket and his hair sticks up as he drags his hand wearily through it. By the time Aman catches up, he has a cigarette firmly in the corner of his lips and his head bowed down to his phone. When he sees Aman he breaks out into a grin, throwing his cigarette onto the ground and stubbing it out with shoe. Sliding his palm against his thigh, he stretches it out towards him and smiles sheepishly.

"That guy was an absolute wanker." His introductory statement takes Aman by surprise, but as he slips his hand into the strangers, he finds the strength and warmth it emanates more surprising. He laughs as they shake hands before their hands return to the safety of their respective jean pockets.

"Nick." He grins as he slides his phone into his pocket and gives his undivided attention to Aman. The boy falters, in university he didn't need to reinvent himself, people took the time to learn the soft 'A' at the beginning of his name.

"Aman." He settles and watches as Nick tests his name by breathing it out. It sounds wonderful falling from his lips, the soft hum of the 'N' at the end of his naming vibrating through him.

Slowly their friendship evolved, their seats in 'World Relations' became closer and closer, until Nick and Aman sat beside one another. They'd debate together, voices united as they spoke, points trailing and linking to one another until the pair dominated the discussion. Notes were traded (with Nick's particularly detailed drawing of a penis sketched into the corner whenever the 'wanker' from the first lecture spoke).

It's a Friday in the autumn term, orange stains the leaves and drags them to the ground around them. Aman wraps a scarf tightly around his neck, longing for the warm Chai that his mother would make for him. Nick fumbles with his hat and pulls it down to cover his ears.

"It must be hard for you, listening to all that bull." Nick suddenly says as they cross the road to a coffee shop, but Aman simply furrows his brows.

"Why would it be particularly hard for me?" He asks, the double meaning not going amiss by Nick who snorts before reverting back to seriousness.

"You know because you're..." He trails off and Aman's lips form an 'O' in realization.

"I'm not Muslim Nick, but my stance isn't because of religion. It's because of my humanity."

NICK ROSTER WAS MADE OF ICE.

He sits in Aman's two bedroom flat, grumbling at the 'crappy English weather.' Aman laughs from the kitchen, whilst he watches the bubbling pot on the stove. It's second nature for him as he places cardamom and clove into the pot, the water sizzling and spitting as he pours in milk.

Soon he returns to his best friend, placing the mug into his hands, before collapsing heavily onto the sofa.

"Ew, I'll pass." Nick states, wrinkling his nose at the foreign smell. Aman rolls his eyes as he grabs the remote and flicks through the channels.

"Shut up and drink it." Aman turns to see Nick yanking his beanie over his head before taking a tentative sip. His initial distaste was replaced by a small smile.

Nick is cut from shards of ice; freezing to touch as Aman brushes against his skin. He is stubborn as he attempts to leave the flat, but Aman stops him and reminds him that he'll just get sicker

"Cheers mate." He manages from under the cocoon of blankets and pillows as Aman straightens up from the electric heater he had just put on.

"Get some sleep you idiot." Aman says affectionately. He heads toward the door, stopping briefly to send a soft look towards his best friend, before returning to his own room.

Their lives become more entwined, paths crossing and meeting until they practically walk side by side. Nick lays on his sofa, ginger hair messy on his freckled hair as he frowns. He faces the window, where snow falls thickly outside. The first term of their third year is nearly over and the campus is full of mistletoe and Christmas trees, the seasonal glow casting a warmth within the students.

"I hate winter." Nick grumbles, his feet resting on the portable heater that he has come to love so dearly.

"You hate the cold." Aman says, his glasses fogging up as he eats his noodles from their plastic container.

"Same thing, ain't it?" Aman simply rolls his eyes, pulling the corner of the blanket from Nick's grasp and curling into it. They huddled together as the small laptop on the coffee table began the TV show. As one episode turned to two and two turned to six, Nick eventually had his head resting against Aman's shoulder and their thighs pressed against each other.

Nick Roster may have been made of ice, but his skin was warm to the touch. Aman frowned as he tried to concentrate on the show, but his focus reverted back to the redhead beside him.

The way his soft hair tickled the crook of his neck.

The way his body curved into his side.

The way his soft sighs would brush against his skin, raising the fine hairs on the back of his arms.

The episode ended and Aman couldn't be happier. Because he didn't understand why the mere feel of Nick's body against his awoke more feelings within him than all the girls that he had with him and under him. Their bodies under his control. He thought of the coil in his stomach, rusting due to its lack of use, and how right now it had been pulled tighter than ever before.

Aman shrugged his shoulder, gently trying to pry himself away. But he didn't realize just how close they were.

Or that when Nick would look up, his green flecked eyes would flicker from his screen, the emeralds glowing brighter than any jewel. His light breaths would hit his chin, fanning over his bronze complexion and flushing his cheeks the same rosy color of his lips.

Their eyes are on one another, running over the slopes of the others noses and the lines of their jaws. That's until Nick stretches out to put a tentative hand to his jaw. Then he presses his lips to Aman's.

AMAN SINGH WAS MADE OF MISTAKES.

Nick's lips are warm, unlike his fingertips that slide into his hair. Each caress sends a shiver down his body, until his knuckles are white as he clenches his fist He doesn't want to give into the way Nick's nose brush and eyelashes flutter against his skin. He doesn't want to melt under the gentle caress that he feels at his waist, as he is readjusted to face Nick fully.

But he can't help it. He can't help the way his lips part to let Nick into his mouth; his tongue languidly stroking his own. Somehow his hand has settled on Nick's waist, fingers splayed out on the small of his back whilst his thumb strokes the front of his stomach. Another hand rises to his hair, the ginger locks so soft and he almost moans at the feel. The strands are like silk engulfing his fingers as they trail up the back of his head.

All too soon, they are parting and Aman wants to reach out and pull him back, but realizes he is the one who is retreating.

"W-we shouldn't have... Fuck- I shouldn't have-" Aman rambles, his hand flying to his hair that had been lingered over by the boy before him, but right now they were being tugged, hard enough to rip it out of his skull.

"Aman." Nick says his name and Aman feels his heart rip, the tendons snapping at the despair in his voice. "Aman, stop." He whispers as Aman tugs at his hair and scrubs his lips with the back of his hand. The light bruising left by Nick is replaced by a self-inflicted darker shade, the hue likening to the ones formed when knuckles bury deep into skin.

"Aman, please." Nick pleads, standing up as well, one hand placed onto Aman's shoulder and the other on his neck. His forehead rests against the boys, and he inhales deeply. When he opens his eyes, he sees wide eyes before him.

Wide with fear.

So he brushes their lips against each other once more, before heading out of the door.

And that was when Aman Singh understood the pain of love. He visits home and his parents gush over his grades, worry over his weight and love his soul. But he feels like an outcast, because the same lips that brushed against his mother's cheeks were pressed against his best friends. Yet to Aman, both seemed right.

Aman thinks he made a mistake, and that they could be rectified with redemption and praying for forgiveness. His hands are clasped together as he bows down, his head covered and his fingers slide the notes down into a tray. His head presses against the carpet and under his breath he mutters the pray his mother repeated night after night when he was younger.

Then he prays for forgiveness.

I'm sorry that I kissed a boy and that it felt so right.

There are no lies with God, no aversion of the truth when faced with an Almighty Deity, so he is truthful. He asks to stop remembering the smooth planes of the boy's body, with his freckles lining his cheeks and unruly ginger hair. He asks to forget his best friend.

When he returns home, the air has shifted and there is a girl in his front room. Their horoscopes are matched and his parents hold hands, hearts filled with hope as they watch the duo. Her eyes are wide and her smile is fake, he notes this down in his mind. A glass is thrust into his hand and he drinks to sedate the drought his throat has subjected itself to. When the adults leave and the girl is left with him, he finds himself looking away. His eyes are trained on the clock to her right when he speaks, his voice low and cold.

"I can't marry you." He doesn't want to see the disappointment in the young girl's eyes, a feeling that will be amplified in both his parent's hearts and eyes.

She gasps, the first tear falling from her eyes and he looks up to see them rolling down her round cheeks at a faster rate. "Thank you." She whispers, the fear of anyone hearing forcing their voices to be lowered. "Thank you." She repeats again and again, her hands shaking and her chest heaving as she sobs. His humanity is what drives him to help her, an arm wrapped her petite frame. When she calms down, she unlocks her phone and shows him a picture.

She stands on a beach, her bikini slipping off her shoulder slightly as she leans into the frame with a man next to her. His ebony arm wraps around her waist and they smile so widely that the sun is thrown onto the back burner while they take the spotlight. His lips are pressed against her cheek and she beams into the camera, wrapped up in love and lust. "I love him." She whispers and Aman holds her close as she sobs into his chest.

Because Aman isn't the first and won't be the last, and neither will she. The door will be held wide open for a wife, even though Aman tries hard to deadbolt it every day.

"Promise me," She whispers, her eyes flickering to the door before training onto his, "promise me, that when you fall in love. You don't let any ties hold you back, even if you think it's your parachute." The hold that she has on his hand is tight and the intensity of her gaze makes Aman stumble to his feet, leaving the room with the stranger. He brushes past his mother, heading straight for the deadbolt door.

"I can't marry her Ma, I can't marry any of them."

AMAN SINGH IS ONLY HUMAN.

He rockets down the road, his foot firmly on the accelerator as he grips the steering wheel. Snow hits the windscreen repeatedly, the wipers working overtime to clear his vision. He flies down the motorway and grits his teeth as he approaches his destination. Feet thunder on the stairs as he takes the steps two at a time. His knuckles wrap into a fist as he bangs on the door, and then it is swinging open.

He stands with a baggy Christmas jumper that has a crude joke about 'baubles' on the front. His hair sticks up, the late night on Christmas Eve taking its toll on the boy. Aman breathes heavily, his eyes flickering up towards the mistletoe above them before settling on Nick. They are toe to toe. Centuries ago, their ancestors stood in the same position, eyes trained on the other, ready to destroy each other. Their swords sought blood and flesh, their minds seeking revenge. As Nick Roster and Aman Singh face each other, they prepare for another battle.

With one last breath, Aman launches himself at the boy. Their actions are carnal; hands gripping, pulling at clothes to bring the other closer. Their lips collide, teeth clinking against each other as they let their tongues tangle messily. His blood stained fingers are marred red with the color of Nick's' hair, clutching it desperately as Nick holds him just as close by his waist. He is free falling without a parachute and he has never felt more alive. Blood rushes around his body and his heart beats twice as fast due to the boy his lips are caressing.

Aman Singh isn't gold. He isn't a question nor a puzzle. Neither is he an object to admire for only it's beauty.

Aman Singh isn't fire. Nick Roster isn't ice.

Aman Singh isn't a mistake.

***AMAN SINGH IS A HUMAN BOY, IN LOVE WITH
A HUMAN BOY NAMED NICK ROSTER.***

Nia Tipton

Nia Tipton was raised in New York City, where she lived until moving to Chicago to attend Columbia College Chicago. She just finished her first year with a major in creative writing and a minor in music business. Nia started writing in the seventh grade, and

one of her favorite books is, *My Heart and Other Black Holes* by Jasmine Warga. She is a lover of French Bulldogs and Frank Ocean.

Life in Color
By Sarah Vita

Gavin sauntered through the revolving door of his new apartment building that was in reality, very old and outdated. Day 25 of job hunting has proven to resemble the last 24 days of job hunting; unsuccessful. He was exhausted both mentally and physically from being denied at each and every place he entered seeking any position they had to offer. Restaurants, clothing stores, grocery markets, even the gas station wasn't hiring any clerks to mind the cubicle sized convenience store. Gavin's confidence was almost depleted and his hopes of finding a new job were fading quickly. His previous job at Webster bank was all Gavin knew, as his father had connections and got him the job right out of college. Webster bank was a well renowned and quite prestigious banking establishment centrally located in downtown Boston. Gavin's degree in accounting and marketing from Boston University helped of course, but it was more his father's inside knowledge that landed him the job at such a young age. The bank was a nice job. It paid the bills and was not physically demanding, a quality Gavin was very thankful for. However, the bank endured the short end of the budget cuts made by the city, leaving 30 of its employees without jobs at the beginning of the New Year. As he walked out of Webster Bank and onto the street on his last day, Gavin felt as if he was a newborn bird, dropped from his nest before learning to fly. Suddenly, everything looked different; the sidewalk, the people, the surrounding buildings all seemed so foreign. He was experiencing what he so fortunately missed out on for the early portion of his life; the struggles of finding a job. January 2nd, 2017 was the beginning of Gavin's new life, and so far it was not going so well.

Gavin rode the squeaky elevator to the fourth floor and released the lock on his apartment door, stepping into the emptiness that was his new home. He had been forced to downsize from his glorious penthouse apartment overlooking the bay as the expenses were too exorbitant without the bank's paycheck. The new one-room apartment resided more inland, with no balcony and a view of other apartment buildings. He sold most of his furniture and appliances on eBay to pay off his old apartment and begin the lease on the new one, so Gavin was essentially broke. His apartment was comprised of his bed, a small armchair with a side table, and a severely under-furnished kitchen. Gavin took a Bud Light from the refrigerator and sank into his armchair, staring at the window as he had no television anymore. He popped open the can and took a long swig, trying to wash out the bad memories of the day and the 24 days that proceeded.

"I can't keep living like this," he thought. "It's pathetic; a successful man like myself resorting to the lifestyle of a hobo. I should be going out, meeting new people, attending parties and events as a representative of Webster Bank. Screw the budget cuts, I shouldn't have been one of them, they need me, they'll see soon enough and beg me to come back."

Gavin had fantasies of Mark Dempsey, CEO of Webster Bank on his hands and knees begging for him to return to the bank. Of course, the bank was running smoothly since Gavin had been let go and there was a computer taking his place which ensured accuracy and required no paycheck. Gavin knew deep down he would not be getting his job back, but imagining his boss begging him to return boosted his confidence ever so slightly. Gavin felt a surge of determination roll over his body. He marched out of his apartment with purpose yet no specific destination in mind. Gavin pushed through the revolving door and into the brisk winter air. He embraced the cold temperature as he made his way down the street. He came upon a new flyer stapled to the telephone pole at the corner of West 8th and 246th St. The notice read "TAG SALE: ALL MUST GO, LOW PRICES! 38 Greene Lane 10am-4pm"

Gavin was surprised in his particular interest in this tag sale, as he wouldn't have given the flyer a second look when he was employed at Webster. He immediately hailed a cab at the corner and headed out to 38 Greene Lane, which luckily happened to be right on the outskirts of the city, so the cab ride wasn't costly.

The cab pulled up outside a small yellow house with black shutters and a white picket fence separating the lawn and sidewalk.

There were a few other people poking around the boxes of items as Gavin surveyed the scene. He paid the cab driver, got out of the car, and made his way to the driveway where the tag sale was being held. Gavin picked up a toaster with a label reading $15.00, and a set of plates with matching silverware priced at $10.00. He felt a sense of accomplishment and success finding these items at such low costs. He wandered the tag sale a little longer to try and decipher which person was the owner of the items, so he could pay for them. An older woman with shiny grey hair and a friendly smile approached him.

"Finding everything okay?" she asked.

"Yes, I would actually like to purchase these items, is it you I owe?" questioned Gavin.

"Indeed, that would be me, I'm Clare Witten, nice to meet you," said the woman extending her hand.

Gavin maneuvered the toaster and dining set into one arm so he could shake Clare's hand. "Gavin Hayes, nice to meet you too," he responded and used his free hand to dig into his pocket for the crumbled bills.

"Thank you very much," Clare said. "I am cleaning out my house from my late husband and all the money is going to the children's hospital, so rest assured, your money is being put to good use."

"That's wonderful!" Gavin exclaimed. He surprised himself with the genuine enthusiasm in his voice, a sound he hadn't heard in a long time.

"Have a nice day Mrs. Witten, and thank you for the items." Gavin turned to walk down the driveway.

She called out, "Please take a painting before you leave, they're very lovely but I have no use for them all now." There was a stack of paintings leaning against the white picket fence at the end of the driveway by the sidewalk. Gavin considered pretending not to hear Mrs. Witten, or give her a smile and politely decline, but her genuine courtesy and kind heart made him reconsider. He leaned down to examine the paintings and selected a small garden scene of bright greens and vivid purple tones. He smiled and waved to Mrs. Witten who was still watching him, and began to walk down the street, completely forgetting that his new apartment wasn't exactly walking distance. Somehow he didn't mind the crisp air or the bulky items in his arms. Gavin embraced the walk back to his apartment which took half an hour and left him quite exhausted after he unloaded the toaster, dining set, and painting onto the kitchen counter. The afternoon escaped Gavin as the premature darkness of late winter arrived and he found himself online job searching in total darkness. He made toast in the toaster which worked well for its age and afterwards headed off to bed.

Gavin rubbed the sleep from his eyes, squinting at his phone on his bedside table that read 9:28 am. The morning light shined through the cracks in the ripped window shade, making it difficult to sleep in. Gavin pulled himself upright in his bed. He noticed the painting from Mrs. Witten's tag sale still on the counter and admired its vivid details. He decided he would hang it above his bed to brighten up the room and bring some happiness to his bland, dull apartment. Days past, Gavin continued his attempts at seeking out a job with no success. His hopeful demeanor was steadily diminishing, leaving him ready to give up. One evening, as Gavin was climbing into bed, he stared at the painting from Mrs. Witten's tag sale, wondering what the painter was thinking when creating the piece. Was he replicating his own garden? Was he using his creative artist imagination to paint his feelings? Who even was the painter? Gavin examined the picture closer than before, searching for a signature or initial indicating the painter's name.

There was no name, initial, date, or title on the painting which struck Gavin as peculiar. He took out his phone and typed a brief description into Google in an attempt to identify the title or artist. "Garden scene of purple flowers", Google produced 5,000 results in 0.5 seconds, all of which were accompanied by an image resembling Gavin's vague description. He scrolled through the results; reviews of paintings, gallery links, and similar images, but none were an exact match to his painting. There were multiple links regarding a highly desired original painting by a famous artist named Claude Monet. Gavin surveyed the links and chose one out of curiosity as to what this prized painting looked like. The image loaded and just as quickly as the painting appeared on the screen, Gavin's jaw dropped. There, illuminated on his phone screen was the painting hung above his bed beside an article entitled "Bid for original copy of Monet's *Garden Oasis* raised to 3.3 million." This could not be true. Gavin refreshed his phone multiple times and rubbed his eyes to ensure that the painting hanging above his bed in his one-room apartment was an original piece worth millions of dollars. It took a few minutes for the reality to set in, but Gavin knew this had to be his big break. All of the bad luck he had experienced in the last few months vanished. He could become a millionaire now and make a life for himself. Gavin deflated into his mattress and drifted off to sleep dreaming of the endless opportunities he would have if this painting was in fact, the original.

Daylight broke and Gavin's eyes shot open, full of positivity and optimism. He got dressed and took the painting off the wall, heading straight for the art gallery on 52nd street where he entered the gallery and made a beeline for the nearest employee.

"Hello, my name is Gavin Hayes and I have a painting I think you would like to see," he announced enthusiastically. The art salesman barely turned to face Gavin before he started speaking.

"Sir we only examine pieces by appointment, you're going to have to…" the man paused, eyes widening as if he had just encountered a ghost.

"G-garden Oasis" he stuttered. "That is the original Monet—do you know what that is worth?!" he demanded. Gavin proudly presented the painting, getting the reassurance he was looking for that he was a soon-to-be millionaire. The art clerk's name was Martin and he took Gavin into a conference room in the back of the gallery. Martin explained that the Monet piece should be auctioned off immediately, as there would be an abundance of prestigious art collectors eager to lay their hands on it. Not only would it bring good press to the gallery, but potential for new business as the art collectors would be exposed to the other pieces on display. The auction was scheduled for the next afternoon and Martin contacted all local as well as out of state galleries extending an invitation. Gavin left the painting in a vault in the gallery and thanked Martin for his help, leaving the gallery feeling like a new man.

The next day, Gavin rounded the corner of 52nd street to an overflowing crowd filling the entirety of the block and an even larger crowd congregating outside of the art gallery. He struggled through the crowd and pushed through the glass doors to find Martin, eager to begin the highly anticipated and very well attended auction. Men in expensive suits, women with floppy hats all holding numbers gathered around a small stage set in the center of the gallery. The Monet was presented on a stand and beside it, a podium with a microphone and Martin standing behind it.

"Behold, the original Claude Monet *Garden Oasis* in mint condition, ready to be auctioned off to the highest bidder. We will begin the bidding at $5,000," Martin pronounced in a very professional tone.

"$15,000" exclaimed an eager voice coming from a man in the front of the crowd.

"$20,000, $30,000, $50,000" voices echoed around the gallery each proclaiming a higher bid than the previous. The numbers continued to rise and before Gavin could even process the amount of money being offered, the bid was up to $2.5 million. Gavin was utterly amazed. He had never imagined his life changing this drastically and in such a short amount of time. He envisioned himself on a tropical island, coconut in hand staring out to the crystal clear blue water. He envisioned a completely furnished apartment that made his old penthouse look like a closet. Gavin snapped back to reality when he heard Martin yell "SOLD to the man in the navy Christian Dior suit for $3.6 million".

Gavin had to realign his stance to prevent himself from falling over. "$3.6 million" he thought to himself. The crowd clapped quietly and a small murmur arose as the bidders dispersed throughout the gallery. The man in the navy suit proceeded towards the stage with an unwavering smile on his face that almost looked childish for someone of his prestige. He approached Gavin. "Emilio Carvelli, pleased to make your acquaintance. I am thrilled you have come forward with this Monet piece, I cannot express how ecstatic I am to have it in my collection now," Emilio's smile was still ear to ear as he spoke.

"I am glad you like it, I trust you'll take good care of it," Gavin said, unsure if that was a fit response as he was not an art collector himself.

"I will have the money transferred to your account within the next two days, I'll just need your bank information" Emilio said to Gavin.

Gavin gladly relayed his bank information over to Emilio and shook his hand again before parting ways. Gavin walked back to his apartment, relishing in the glory that he was about to encounter once the money reached his almost empty bank account. He immediately began searching for a new apartment online and searched "most luxurious island getaways" on Google. By the end of the night, Gavin had vacations planned for the next 6 months, traveling Europe, exploring Asia, and venturing south of the border where he could work on his tan. When Emilio's money reached Gavin's account a day later, the trips were booked and Gavin was off. He immersed himself in new cultures and met all different types of people, embracing his newfound wealth the best way he could think of. Gavin lived a life of luxury for months, worry and care free. He visited the Colosseum, the rainforest, even the Taj Mahal; places Gavin had never dreamed of seeing in person. While wandering the streets of Rome one sunny summer afternoon, Gavin happened upon an open air market and decided to stroll through it. He browsed handmade jewelry, candles, some cheesy tourist souvenirs, but stopped at a table showcasing hand-blown glass ornaments and figurines. They were so delicate and vibrant in their bright colored designs. An old woman sat behind the table and gave Gavin a soft smile, inducing a strong feeling of déjà vu that Gavin could not pinpoint. Puzzled, he continued to walk, wondering why that woman looked so familiar. He was sure he had never seen her before, yet she reminded him of someone so distinctly. Mrs. Witten.

Gavin stopped in his tracks. Mrs. Witten, the kind old woman who insisted he take a painting from her tag sale. The woman who lost her husband and was donating all the money she made from the tag sale to the children's hospital. Gavin's mind raced wondering how he could have forgotten about Mrs. Witten. Did she know that the painting was an original? Had she heard that Gavin auctioned it off and became rich? Questions he could not answer swarmed his mind and he suddenly felt suffocated with guilt and devastation. He had to go back to her house and give her a proper apology and explanation. Gavin would give Mrs. Witten a significant portion of the money he still had left to make up for his terrible mistake. She deserved the money. Mrs. Witten was so genuine and gentle and Gavin had unconsciously taken advantage of her, wrapped up in wealth and materialistic endeavors. He booked the next flight out and returned home to set things straight.

The cab pulled up in front of the little yellow house with the black shutters. The white picket fence was showing signs of age but overall the house looked the same as it had a few months ago. Gavin sauntered to the front door dragging his feet, feeling weighted down by guilt. He rang the doorbell, his palms were sweaty as his nerves increased. A young woman opened the door. She had light brown hair and brown eyes. She gave Gavin a peculiar look and said, "Hello I am Emma Witten, what can I do for you?"

"My name is Gavin Hayes and I bought something from Mrs. Clare Witten's tag sale a few months back that I'd like to talk to her about. Is she home?" Gavin questioned.

"I am sorry if you were a friend of my mothers, but she passed a month ago from her battle with breast cancer" Emma's facial expression deepened and her eyes filled with tears.

Gavin felt as if he had been struck by a car. He felt paralyzed, unable to move or speak.

"Oh no" was all that escaped his lips.
"I am so sorry, may I come in? I have some explaining to do." Gavin knew he needed to tell Emma everything to clear his conscience. He felt as if it were the right thing to do. Emma invited him in and they sat at the kitchen table. The house was a mess, boxes everywhere filled with items.

"Excuse the mess" Emma said. "I am cleaning out the house in preparation for it to be put on the market."

"Oh it's no problem. I am so sorry about your mother," Gavin said, meaning it wholeheartedly.

He explained the story start to finish and Emma listened attentively and patiently as Gavin choked back tears. His eyes stung and his bottom lip was quivering as he spoke, but he did not care.

When he finally stopped speaking he realized he was sobbing. Emma was quiet for a while then softly said "I understand."

Gavin was unsure if that was a reassuring statement or angered response to his story.

"I forgive you, it's okay" Emma continued. "You sound like a really nice person and making the effort to correct your mistake is very honorable of you."

Gavin's body relaxed slightly. He still felt incomplete and dissatisfied with Emma's acceptance of his apology. Gavin felt a sense of responsibility for Mrs. Witten's death. If he had given her the money from the painting immediately, could she have been saved? Would the money have helped to pay for more treatment or medicine? Would Mrs. Witten be alive today if he had given back the painting once he discovered its worth? Again, questions Gavin could not answer. All Gavin knew for certain was that he had wronged Mrs. Witten and she did not deserve the fate she received. Gavin felt a powerful connection to Mrs. Witten and her family despite not knowing her at all. Days past and the feelings of guilt and regret only grew stronger. What could Gavin do to relieve himself of these emotions? He could not spend his life feeling this plaguing remorse. Then, the idea hit him.

The Clare Witten Cancer Research Foundation was born almost a year after Gavin had attended the tag sale. He used the money from the Monet painting to jumpstart the organization as fast as possible. Gavin devoted his life to this organization to fund research towards finding a cure for breast cancer. Also, Gavin linked the organization to the children's hospital where Mrs. Witten volunteered and donated her tag sale earnings to them. Emma joined as Vice President of the organization, helping Gavin plan events and raise awareness both locally and nationwide. Gavin's life had a new meaning, and his perspective shifted from self-centered to open-minded, embracing each day as another opportunity to help others. Gavin knew that this was the path he was destined to take, and Mrs. Witten would be proud of him. Her kind heart would never be forgotten, and Gavin had Mr. Claude Monet to thank for that.

Sarah Vita

Spending a semester abroad in Florence, Italy proved to be more than just pasta and pizza for author Sarah Vita. Sarah is an Education major and English minor, aspiring to be a third grade

teacher and writer on the side. Upon graduation in one short year, Sarah will pursue a Master's degree in Education and hopefully land a job where she can specialize in teaching Language Arts, as her passion is to teach children to love reading and writing as she did/still does. Going abroad, writing for her school's online blog, and keeping a journal has helped Sarah strengthen her writing skills. Her inspiration stems from genuine, relatable experiences or events whether abroad, at school, in her small hometown of Hamden, Connecticut, or her favorite escape on Cape Cod. However, creative writing has always been an enjoyable stress reliever and mode of expression for her. This is her first publication, though definitely not her last as she returns to Merrimack College for her senior year.

Critical Nonconformity
By Connor J. Walcott

In the year 2080, human civilization was on the brink of
collapse. Widespread and increasingly violent civil unrest, coupled
with the ever-present threat of an impending global war, had crippled
the world economy. Disease, starvation, and death were rampant,
reducing the people of even the strongest nations to little more than
miserable, paranoid animals.

In one last desperate attempt to find a solution, the few
remaining world leaders assembled an international coalition
consisting of the best and brightest historians, sociologists,
neuroscientists, psychologists, and philosophers. This group existed
for one purpose and one purpose only: to find a way to prevent
mankind from tearing itself apart.

Months, then years, were spent searching, to no avail. Despite
the countless hours spent studying every society that ever existed,
every survey ever conducted, every cultural treatise ever written, the
team found themselves continually arriving at one simple yet
seemingly inescapable conclusion: conflicts occur because people are
different. All warfare resulted from differences between nations,

social conflicts from differences between groups, crime from differences between individuals. The infinite number of social and cultural variables that made up human existence always resulted in an unpredictable combination unique to every person, making the idea of a completely unified global society altogether impossible, as unattainable as it was optimistic.

Then, in 2084, nearly four years to the day after the task force was created, a breakthrough, a solution as beautifully simple as the problem itself: if people were incapable of ever truly settling their differences, *why not eliminate the differences altogether?*

And so, a radical new approach to human society was developed, designed to abolish the causes of all suffering, all hardship, all conflict, forever.

They called their idea *Conformity*.

The driving principle behind Conformity was simple: when everyone is the same, everyone is equal.

One by one, the few nations with still-intact governments began to restructure themselves, adjusting to accommodate the new world order. Desperate for any sort of relief from the horror that daily life had become, the common people wholeheartedly accepted Conformity and embraced it as the cultural savior it claimed to be. Within a few short decades, the world seemed well on its way to attaining the global utopia of which it had long dreamed.

Now, nearly a century later, the power of Conformity is absolute. War, crime, and poverty have all been eradicated. The past and its horrors are now nothing more than unpleasant memories, pushed into the dustiest corners of the collective consciousness.

Everyone is safe—everyone is happy—everyone is equal—and above all,

Everyone is the same…

*****

At precisely 6:30 a.m., the blaring alarm of the digital clock on the bedside table roused John from sleep, just as it did every morning. The alarm automatically cut itself off after ten chimes, but it was enough; John had been up after the first one.

Rising slowly from the bed, John stretched his stiff muscles and shuffled across the gray tile floor towards the bathroom, rubbing the sleep from his eyes. His approach tripped the motion-activated light switch mounted on the wall, and the worn LED ceiling fixture flickered to life, illuminating the cramped bathroom. Squinting against the sudden light, John made his way towards the sink against the far wall.

As he neared the counter, yet another sensor activated, opening the tap and filling the sink with water. Cupping his hands under the running faucet, John splashed the still-cold water onto his face, washing away the last traces of sleep. As the water ran down his face, he looked into the stainless mirror, taking in the details of his reflection

Face and head totally bald save for a day's worth of black stubble across his chin and scalp. Eyes a light brown, small flecks of green around the pupils. Thin-lipped mouth that naturally pulled itself into a small half-smile at the corners. A face of perfect ethnic ambiguity, with skin neither too dark nor too pale, features belonging to every race and none simultaneously. Perfectly symmetrical, perfectly proportioned, perfectly…average.

Which was exactly what Conformity had intended when, fifty-odd years ago, it had become the face of every living human being on the planet.

In the earliest stages of Conformity's implementation, an independent group of scientists had a breakthrough of their own. After decades of research, they successfully mapped the entirety of the human genome, finally gaining an understanding of the basic building-blocks of human life. It had initially begun as an attempt to eradicate birth defects and childhood illness, thereby strengthening the human race. A few simple rounds of prenatal gene therapy, and out came a perfectly healthy child, every single time, guaranteed. Of course, it hadn't taken long for the new Conformist government to discover a far more useful application for the new discovery—the ability to directly control which physical characteristics a newborn child would manifest, picking and choosing the ones they deemed most beneficial to their new society. An opportunity of this magnitude was simply too tempting to pass up, and so the practice of genetically altering unborn children had been adopted as one of Conformity's greatest traditions. The result had been an entire generation of fully-functional children, perfectly normal…and perfectly identical.

After a few generations, the changes made to the gene sequence became permanent, allowing the attention of Conformity's overseers to be directed elsewhere. The final members of the pre-Conformity generation had died off over forty years ago, and with them died the final traces of the world that came before. All that remained was a population of several billion people who looked exactly like John.

Guess they're lucky I'm so damn handsome, John quipped silently to himself, the joke dying before it could reach his lips.

The sound of the faucet shutting off pulled John's attention away from his reflection. The sink, now filled with lukewarm water, stood ready for the daily shaving which Conformity demanded of its citizens

Too bad they couldn't bother to edit out hair growth, John thought bitterly. *Could have saved us all a lot of time in the morning.*

As usual, the thought went unspoken.

As he reached out with his right hand to pick up the razor from the sink, the familiar shimmer of the blue light on the inside of his wrist caught his eye. There, barely noticeable under the bright overhead light, was a two-inch long barcode, the lines glowing a faint blue just beneath the skin. Directly below that, in tiny blue letters, was the code C-137.

This code, those four simple digits, defined everything about who John was as a person. As had been discovered close to a century ago, names implied some inherent variation from person to person—a concept the principles of Conformity simply could not allow. So, naturally, names had been abolished altogether, and every citizen was now simply known as "John" or "Jane," depending on their gender, with the codes taking the place of surnames and serving as the government's way of properly documenting their citizens.

Of course, the code's existence would have been impossible if not for the tiny subcutaneous device that projected it: the Filter, crowning achievement of Conformist society.

Not long after the completion of the gene-altering process, the government had encountered a second major setback: despite their initial success in ensuring that every citizen *looked* the same, they had simply been unable to force them all to *think* the same. Even with the countless breakthroughs in science and medicine the past decades had brought, the secret to suppressing human ingenuity and creativity had proven frustratingly elusive.

Then, as always, another breakthrough: If science was unable to eliminate human capacity for nonconformist thoughts, then it could at least remove the capacity to act upon them.

Thus, the Filter, perhaps the greatest—and ultimately the final—piece of human engineering was produced: a tiny, pill-shaped device, implanted in the wrist at birth, which allowed for a complete reprogramming of the brain's interaction with the rest of the body. Now, any and all neurological signals sent to any part of the body were first processed through the Filter, and checked against a predetermined list of properly Conformist behaviors before approval. Acceptable actions were allowed to continue, while unacceptable ones were stopped short, or, in some cases, substituted with more "appropriate" ones.

With the introduction of the Filters, the human mind was stripped of its last bit of autonomy, becoming nothing more than a prisoner trapped for a lifetime in a cage of flesh and bone, forced to observe and interpret the outside world as it saw fit, but with no ability whatsoever to influence it.

John's brain hated that cage with a burning passion that filled every moment, waking or sleeping, with a restless desire to escape or destroy it.

And most days, he'd have sworn that the cage returned the sentiment.

As if determined to prove his point, John's Filter code blinked red for a brief moment, indicating its detection and subsequent blocking of any anti-Conformity actions or ideas.

John felt his hands robotically begin to shave his face and head, the Conformist programming of the Filter having determined that the stubbly growth was simply unacceptable. It set him apart, and for that reason, it had to be eliminated.

Such a shame, really, he thought, as he did every morning. *I think I'd look good with a beard.*

As usual, the Filter's only response was a red flash of disapproval.

*****

The drab factory where John worked, with its walls of gray-painted brick and billowing industrial smokestacks, was, of course, a perfect copy of every other factory in the City, the ocean of uninterrupted concrete that stretched across the majority of the continent once known as North America.

As he approached, he fell into line behind the hundreds of other Johns and Janes streaming into the building, each one freshly shaved and dressed in the fitted gray-and-blue jumpsuits issued to all Conformist citizens. As the procession of workers filed in through the yawning mouth of the factory, John caught snippets of the small-talk exchanged by his nearby coworkers…or, at least, what passed for small-talk by Conformity standards. Thanks to the Filters' rigorous censorship subroutines, chit-chat now consisted mostly of innocuous comments about the weather and, in rare cases, a spontaneous utterance of "Praise Conformity!"

And here I was afraid someone would finally have something interesting to say, John thought dryly.

"What wonderful weather we're having," the Filter corrected, red light flashing as it finally broke John's silence for the day.

Noticing the comment, the John in front of him glanced back momentarily, mirroring the vapid half-smile present on John's own face. "It *is* quite mild for this time of year," he said in greeting, then promptly turned around again, resuming the silence.

Once inside, John walked down a series of uniform hallways lined with uniform metal cubicles until finally arriving at his designated station, indicated by the C-137 glowing on the screen of the wall-mounted monitor by the cubicle's doorway. Below that, in the same blue Conformity-approved font, was a digital readout of the time: 8:00 a.m. on the dot.

Rolling up the sleeve of his jumpsuit, John held his Filter code in front of the screen, and the mirrored numbers flashed twice as the Filter connected to the factory's mainframe, clocking him in for the day. In response, the cubicle's pneumatic door slid open and the interior light activated.

Another day, another dollar, John mused as he stepped inside.

In unison, his Filter and its counterpart on the wall flashed a red warning.

"Hard work is its own reward," the Filter substituted.

Right, John thought with a sigh. *Good Conformists don't get paid.*

Shrugging off the thought, he stepped forward, readying himself for the job at hand as, all across the factory, the vast array of machinery churned to life.

At station C-137, John manufactured…well, he wasn't exactly sure. His job consisted of standing in the cubicle in front of a conveyor belt, assembling small rectangular components as they came down the line, undoubtedly placed there by another John or Jane one station over. Each part was placed into a casing of matte-black plastic, held in place with three rivets from the rivet gun in John's right hand, then placed back on the conveyor and transported somewhere else. The process took less than ten seconds per part, and John had repeated it for eleven hours a day, seven days a week, since he'd entered the Conformist workforce nearly twenty years ago.

Yet, despite the years of experience, John still had no idea what the parts actually *did.* For all he knew, the components he was responsible for creating could have been used to build some sort of weapon, or to power air conditioners, or simply dropped into a trash chute and disposed of, with his job serving no purpose other than to occupy his hands for yet another day. Once each part was pulled down the conveyor and through the slot in the cubicle wall, Conformity deemed that it was no longer relevant to the task at hand.

The day passed by as slowly as the countless others before it, the work as mind-numbingly repetitive as always. As his programmed hands moved mechanically through the motions, performing the same task over and over and over again, John let his mind go completely blank, a lifetime of practice allowing him to retreat so far within himself that he no longer thought about anything at all. In moments like these, he surrendered even the faint illusion of individuality his thoughts provided, allowing his programming to accomplish its task unimpeded by even those minor inconveniences.

He had found it was easier that way.

*****

Somewhere overhead, a bell chimed, signifying 7:00 p.m. The end of the work day.

Just like he did every day, John waited as the conveyor slowly ground to a halt, the internal gears humming softly as it did so. After verifying that everything had shut down correctly— rendered redundant by the factory's programming, but still mandated by the Filter—John turned and headed towards the door.

As the door slid open before him, the display screen on the conveyor emitted a small beep, an indicator light flashing.

What the hell? John thought as his body turned towards the sound.

"Nonconformity," John's mouth mumbled quietly, uttering the programmed response to anything that deviated from the norm, which served as equal parts expletive, observation, and accusation.

The display screen flashed a red error code: ERROR CODE 13-7B: CRITICAL NONCONFORMANCE DETECTED.

Even with the Filter's influence, John's face took on a look of confusion. That error code was only supposed to appear when a component was damaged to the point of posing a danger to the entire system. Although his job training had, of course, prepared him for the eventuality of a mechanical failure, John had honestly never expected to encounter one.

John stood frozen in place for a moment as the Filter attempted to determine how to proceed, then moved forward as the compulsion to prevent damage to the machinery overwrote the command to cease working for the day.

Approaching the inactive conveyor and tapping the screen, John opened the error message, quickly scanning the details it provided. His mind was paying full attention now; twenty years on the job, and this was the first remotely interesting thing that had happened. According to the diagnostic report, an electrical cable inside the wall of the cubicle had come loose during the shutdown sequence, causing a loss of connection with the next station and preventing a downline transfer.

John watched as his hand reached towards the opening and disappeared from view inside the wall, searching through the maze of wires and valves to find the loose cable. Although it deviated from the standard behavior, efficiency dictated that the error needed to be corrected, and so the Filter allowed it. Keeping one eye on the monitor, his hand finally located its target, and, using the display as a guide, plugged the cable back into place.

At that moment, before John could withdraw his hand, the conveyor's machinery churned to life, completing the final half-second of the shutdown process. For a moment, he felt an odd tingling in his hand as power surged through the cable in his hand, and then, suddenly, a wave of unimaginable pain coursed through him. Every muscle in his body locked into place, pulling so tightly they threatened to tear themselves apart. As thin tendrils of smoke rose from inside the machine, John's vision began to go dark.

Then, as suddenly as it had begun, the pain vanished, and John slumped to the ground in a heap, his arm pulling free of the wall, singe marks lining his sleeve. He lay awkwardly splayed out on the floor, heart pounding, his breath coming in deep, ragged gasps. Random tingling sensations ran through his body, and the air smelled faintly of acrid smoke.

When feeling finally returned to his extremities, he gingerly sat up and looked around. The clock on the wall now read 7:02. The whole ordeal had lasted less than two minutes.

Slowly rising from the floor, he dusted himself off, ensuring that his limbs had full mobility as he did so, then checked the status of the machinery. All systems, both organic and mechanical, were functioning normally, all indicator lights showing green. Opening the door to his cubicle, he stepped out into the hall, falling in line with the hundreds of other Johns and Janes as they filed out of the factory and onto the City streets, as though nothing had happened.

Just another face in a sea of identical faces.

*****

The Conformity-mandated bedtime was exactly 10:00 p.m., and so, every night, John's Filter directed him towards his bed, regardless of whether he was tired or not.

That evening, as always, John shuffled over to his bed and laid down on his side, facing the bedside table. Staring at the glowing numbers on the clock, John counted down the minutes, as he did every night:

…9:58…9:59…10:00.

Only this time, his eyes didn't close.

Unblinking, he stared at the clock, expecting to suddenly fall asleep.

…10:01…10:02…10:03

Maybe the clock is wrong, he thought.

But the clocks were never wrong. Conformity didn't get things wrong.

…10:04…10:05…10:06.

At exactly 10:07, he slowly sat up in his bed, awake past the curfew for the first time in his life. According to every known law of Conformity, this should have been impossible. Everyone slept at the same time every night. No exceptions. The Filter should have prevented this, forced his body to sleep. The Filter…

With one motion, he threw off the sheets and half-tripped, half-ran to the bathroom, the light activating as he passed. With trembling hands, John pushed up the right sleeve of his jumpsuit, face suddenly paling at what he saw in the light. Where once the Filter code had been a soft blue, it was now permanently locked in the accusatory shade of red reserved for Nonconformist thoughts. Beneath the skin, the pill-like shape of the device visible as a distended bump on his wrist, from which radiated a network of tiny burn marks, forming a pattern like that of a spider's web.

Feeling suddenly sick, he staggered backwards into the bedroom, eyes still fixed in horror at his arm as the truth dawned on him: whatever had happened to him in the factory had deactivated his Filter. He was now the thing that every good citizen feared most: a Nonconformist.

How is this happening? He thought in a panic. *How is this even possible?*

In that moment, sitting there on his bed, alone in the darkness, he faced down the reality that life as he knew it was over. His mind reeled, alternating between total numbness and all-out panic.

Then, out of the chaos of his thoughts, a single revelation—a breakthrough. A simple, beautiful, terrifying, entirely inescapable conclusion.

I'm free.

At first, it seemed almost laughable. Under Conformity, everyone was already free! Suffering of every kind had been eliminated. Equality reigned supreme.

But this…somehow John knew that this was what real freedom felt like, even without ever having experienced it before, as if it had filled a void within him that he hadn't known existed until now.

The more he thought it, the more real it became.

I'm free. I'm finally free.

Time for one final test. Taking a deep, ragged breath, John spoke for the first time in his life. Not the Conformist babbling of the Filter, but his own thoughts, finally put into words, given life at long last.

"I'm free. I'm finally free."

He didn't shout it. There was no need too. It wasn't about how the words were said, just that he was actually able to say them.

He lost track of how many times he said it. Those same words, over and over and over again, each time gaining a new, deeper meaning.

"I'm finally free."

At that moment, every word the Filter had ever censored, every impulse the Filter had ever blocked, came rushing out at once, the pouring out of a lifetime of pent-up thoughts and emotions. Springing up from where he sat, he began pacing erratically around his room, laughing in borderline hysterics, tears streaming down his face in a decidedly Nonconformist display of emotion.

John lost all sense of time, and, in that moment, he found that it didn't matter. All that mattered was that one single instant, and the overwhelming sense of relief it brought with it.

Hours passed, and, eventually, he was interrupted by the sound of an electronic alarm chirping loudly from across the room. Ten chimes. 6:30 a.m. Conformity dictated that it was time for another day at work.

But for the first time in his life, John C-137 didn't care what Conformity wanted.

THE END

Connor J. Walcott

Connor Walcott is a proud life-long resident of Sunrise, Florida, and is currently a senior in the English department at Florida Atlantic University. Following his graduation in the fall of 2018,

Connor plans on pursuing a career in editing and publishing, where his fierce devotion to absolute grammatical correctness can finally be put to good use. His hobbies are as diverse as they are trivial, and include laughing at his own cringe-worthy puns, having in-depth discussions about either politics or superhero movies, and quoting verbatim lines from every movie or TV show he's ever seen. When he's not busy writing, cramming for exams, or volunteering at his local church, Connor can usually be found obsessing over his hair, singing along (completely off-key) to '80's rock music, or relaxing in his favorite recliner with an iced tea in one hand and a video game controller in the other.

The Music Box of Souls
By Cassandra Winnie

I always knew that he liked me, I just didn't think that he would risk everything for me. He was always nice to me. Now that I think of it, he was always *too* nice. I guess I am the fool for not checking his i.d. because now I'm the one without an identity. I am no longer myself and I can never escape. Lesson is don't trust a stranger, even when he claims to be your boss.

I had just moved from Smallville, a tiny town in Texas, to New York. My dancing career was at its peak and I made the *big* move. I was recruited to be a professional ballerina for a dance company called Bad Babes of Ballet. They were preparing to perform a show called the *Black Mystic* and they wanted me to be the lead. I didn't have much family to worry about and this was a big opportunity for me. Besides, how could I give it up? It was a perfect opportunity and the big named dance companies purchased tickets for the show in advance. I knew that if I mastered this part, I could become a star and I was ready to be famous.

The first day of the job, I slipped on my black leotard in my new apartment. My apartment was tiny but it was only a temporary home. If I became lonely, I had my cat, Moody to keep me company.

Moody came with me everywhere and I could not leave him behind. I packed my ballet shoes into a bag and started for the studio. I stepped outside and felt a cool breeze crawl up my back as I ran to the corner.   It was already eight and I had an appointment with my new boss in thirty minutes. I flagged down the first taxi I saw and asked him to drive me to 66 Westwood Ave.

Slowly, opening the door in front of my new work place, a rush of excitement raced through me. I ran up to the door and pulled on the handles but the door wouldn't budge. In the corner of my eye, I saw the taxi driver still staring and I was embarrassed. There was a sign on the door that said, "Calice, please come to the back." I darted around the building to the back door, and immediately got the chills. Directly behind the back door, there was an alley way. It was a dirty little alley, dark as night. Man, it was like the alley in your nightmare that you thought you would get kidnapped in. I saw someone approaching me from the back of the alley so I quickly ran inside.

Entering and calling "hello" my new co-workers were excited to finally meet me. I happened to get this part because the first girl quit or at least they said that she quit. She said that some man kept following her around and coming in the studio and watching her at night. They did not have video cameras so nobody believed her. One day she never came back so they assumed that she quit. The girls gave me all the details about the boss and what I would need to do to impress him. They wanted to introduce me to him but he wasn't there which I thought was strange because I was supposed to meet him to discuss our contract. At least, I thought that was what my email said. I danced with the women as we watched the tapes of this dance from many years ago. I quickly learned the steps to my part in the first dance. Time passed quickly but the boss never came back so the girls said that I could go home.

The other dancers all left but I wanted to work on my part. I stayed after for about two hours, when a dark shadow stood at the door. The spot light was on my face and I couldn't see who it was. I stopped dancing and approached the edge of the stage on the tips of my toes.. The man came forward and said, "Wow. You are amazing, I knew that you were going to be."

"And you are?"

"Oh, I'm sorry, I'm Mark. The owner of this studio."

"Oh my gosh. How silly of me. Hi! I was looking for you everywhere this morning. You canceled our meeting?"

"I had to talk to one of our guards about getting a new alarm system. Some creep keeps coming in or at least that's what our last lead said." I was so thrilled to meet my boss. I could already tell that he was going to love my work ethic and talent. We talked for an hour and he wanted to see my audition routine again. He was very impressed. Mark walked me out that night and paid for my taxi back to my home.

The next day, rehearsal was fantastic. We reviewed all of the steps to our dance and put together the first routine. I was the center of attention and my jumps needed to be on point. Mark didn't come to practice again and I asked the girls were he was. They said that he had been really busy planning the costumes so he usually came at night to lock up the studio. I knew that he would appear later that night and when everyone else left, he did. He told me that he had fired the man that was going to put in the alarm because he put a camera in the girl's dressing room. What a pig.

Mark told me that my jumps looked a little sloppy that night. My left leg was not high enough so he helped me raise it. He stretched my leg out and every time I jumped, he held my hips to lift me. It was a little awkward because he was my boss but I guess he had to touch my hips to help me achieve my goal. He threw me up and we were an inch away from each other's face. When we had finished, we sat outside by the bus stop and took a taxi together. When we approached my building, the cab stopped and I handed my money to Mark. He refused to take it and paid for my taxi again. I felt strange but I was not going to anger my boss, so I left with a smile and a thank you.

I went home to find Moody on top of my kitchen table ripping a plastic wrapper. I trailed it back to my kitchen to find a basket of fruit with a card. It said "Greetings! From Mark and the Bad Babes of Ballet. I am so thrilled to have you as part of my company. Here is a little something to make you feel at home."

Two weeks flew by, and the show was coming up. Mark never came to the practices but always stayed and helped me after everyone had left. In fact, he was very angry when I didn't stay on

Wednesday. He told me that I was going to gain weight if I didn't stay late and work on my solo. I always watched my weight and I did not want to hear his criticism so I left him there alone. Returning home angry and upset, I realized that Moody had disappeared. The windows were closed and the door was locked. I checked under the bed and everywhere a cat could possibly hide but Moody was gone. About thirty minutes later, I heard a ring at the doorbell. I opened the door to find Mark holding Moody. How did he find my cat? Mark told me that he lived in this building too and that he saw a cat wandering the hallway. When he grabbed it, he saw that it said room #136 so he was just bringing him home. I said thanks and went to turn him away but he stuck his foot in my door. He grabbed my face and stared me in the eyes, asking if I was uncomfortable. I denied it but he knew I was lying. He told me that I made him upset but it was the other way around. I asked him again to leave but he made himself comfortable in my home. Mark threw off his shoes and went to my room. He sat on my bed and demanded that I come sit too. "Get over here Cal." When I denied him, hugging my cat, he got up, pulled my arm, and forced me to sit next to him. "You act like I'm creeping you out. Relax." He started kissing my arm and rubbing my shoulders so I got up and asked him to leave. He started yelling at me and calling me disgusting words. He put on his shoes and said, "You better start watching yourself, and the way you talk to me. You don't want to lose your job do you?" Mark slammed the door and I sat and cried holding my Moody.

The next morning, I was in a miserable mood. It was rainy and I was late to work. The girls were asking if I was excited because our show was the next day, but I was not. I felt weird and I did not want to see Mark. Fortunately he was not at our practice again. At the end of the session, I looked down at my busted up ballet shoe. I split it landing a grande jette with too much force. Suddenly I saw Mark at the door. I quickly packed my things in an attempt to flee before he could talk to me. He apologized for acting the way he did and said that he was just very stressed because his wife had left him. Since he acted out, he said that he had gotten me something but I didn't want it. Mark told me that it was from the company so I opened it to find a new pair of black ballet shoes to match my costume. I was so happy because I had not received my check yet to buy a new pair of shoes. My rent was high and every penny went towards the cost of living. These were of the highest line of ballerina shoes. Thank you so much. Since we lived in the same building, we took a taxi together and he once again apologized for acting the way he did. He said it was because I am just really talented and beautiful so we agreed to let it go. He paid for my taxi and walked me to my door. In front of my door, there was another box addressed to me. It said "For the Show, Calice, from Mark and the Girls". I looked down at the present and said, "Another one. You guys! I thought you said that I was getting my costume tomorrow?" I turned around to hear nothing but silence and see nothing but the paintings in the hall. Huh, guess he did not want to see my reaction until tomorrow.

I took my gift inside and opened it. It was a beautiful black shimmering tutu with long black feathers down the back and black shiny beads around the neck. It was elegant and beautiful and the best part was that nobody else was wearing it but me. I wanted to thank Mark for my outfit so I sent him an email. I decided that I would just go to his room and thank him but I didn't know where he lived.

I went to the front desk and asked for his door number. The attendant told me that there was nobody named Mark Neimos here. I then explained how he was my boss and he is famous but the man said "Nope, not in the building." Huh. I went back to my room confused and talked to my cat like a crazy woman.

The day of the show was amazing, everything was perfect. Before performing, I went to the back stage to find a man standing with red luscious roses at my desk. I didn't know who he was so I asked him why he was back here and who he was waiting for.

He said, "It's me."

"Me who?"

"Silly, well we haven't officially met. I'm sorry, I'm Mark. I had to cancel our first meeting due to issues with the police and the alarms. Well you know our last lead never came back so the police have a reason to believe something terrible has happened to her. Anyway, you did such an amazing job so I got you these roses. And I want you in my next show." I started laughing and asked him who he really was. He told me that he was serious. I told him that my boss had been helping me after practice every day. He stared at me in awe.

"I'll prove it." Mark took me to his office and pulled up all of the videos from the new cameras. The film consisted of me dancing with the other Mark. My real boss quickly called the police to take a look at this mysterious man who had been impersonating him. The other girls had no idea what was even going on. I told him that this Mark had been to my apartment so the police were going to meet me there to scan for finger prints. I quickly ran out the back door to avoid the reporters and people in waiting in the front. Running out the back, I tripped and fell into the hands of a man.

"Excuse me, I am terribly sorry." He had a black fedora on covering his eyes and he was wearing a gray petticoat. He slowly released me but feeling a pinch, I looked down to see him pulling a needle out of my shoulder. "What, what is this? I have to… have to go. I need to get…" and that's all I remember, until I woke up hours later in a box

. It was dark, cold, and I was alone. The silence crept over my body as I started to scream for help, but nobody came. My feet were tied to a small platform at the end of the box and my legs were positioned on tiny stilts. I heard footsteps and I yelled for help again. This time I heard a whisper. "Shhh. You're going to destroy the show." Suddenly, I heard a cranking noise and the lid of the box opened. I could not move but my body was positioned like a ballerina and I suddenly rose up standing inside the box. I was on a spring like contraption in a large music box. The sad soft tune began to play and I slowly rotated looking into a mirror 0n the inside of the lid. Behind me in the mirror was the man who had called himself *Mark*. His eyes were filled with lust and desire. He grabbed my face and kept kissing me. I tried to fight him but he shot me again with a needle. "I just could not let you go Calice. I had to have you."

"Please let me go. You can come to my shows and I'll let you sit in the front. I won't tell anybody I promise. It can be our secret."

"No! Now you are my ballerina. You will dance for me when I want to see you. You will love me when I want you to love me and you will respect me."

"Please, people are going to miss me. You are going to get caught. The…the real Mark will be looking for me!"

"Right. Just like they are looking for Rosette?"

"Who is Rosette?" He pointed to another box about the size of the one I was being contained in. It was locked and dusty. I looked at his face but he didn't care. He smirked like my question was humorous. I was horrified and disgusted. "Is she in there? Is she alive?" He never answered me. I asked him a few more times and started to cry but he only enjoyed my misery.

"Who is looking for you? Mark will find another star for me. And you? A little country girl, starting a job in the big city. A little nobody with no family support. Nobody will even notice that you are gone." Emotionally exhausted, I heard mumbles and my eyes rolled back inside my head. I had fainted again.

I tried to escape so many times, but it was impossible. I came to realize that it was not worth the effort or the energy. He locked my music box every night and he changed my costumes every day. He drugged me, brushed my hair, and took care of me the way a neglectful mother would care for her child. He wanted me to be "perfect" so sometimes he didn't feed me. Other times, he took advantage of my body or left me in the box untouched for days. Sometimes if I was lucky, he made me dance three times a day. I was *Mark's new toy*. The police never looked for me, at least I don't think they did. Nobody came to rescue me and the dance studio shut down without me. Life had stopped all around me. I never should have moved to New York. Next time, if there is a next time, I will make sure people are who they say they are. I will never trust a stranger again. I now listen to the sad soft tune that chimes from my music box. Staring through the key hole and crying into the night, hoping that somebody can hear my sobs.

Cassandra Winnie

Cassandra Winnie believes that writing is a cure for a troubled soul. Writing has become such a gift in her life and an important therapeutic element. She will be attending NYU for her master's

degree in social work. While helping others heal, she also hopes to continue encouraging and inspiring others to write their story because as Maya Angelou once said, "There is no greater agony than bearing an untold story inside of you." Cassandra is a New Jersey resident and has a passion for poetry.

Deep Purple
By Jamie Sharon Wright

No one knows what a kidnapper looks like. Except me. I know exactly what a kidnapper looks like. She is short and soft and has blond hair that bounces just shy of her shoulder blades, though she thinks it's ugly. Dirty dishwater blonde is what color she calls it, but I think it's gorgeous. She has blue eyes the color of cloudless skies. She's the president of the PTA and shows up to every sports game and music event and school play. She's the reason when I come home from school, there's always cookies on the table, fresh from the oven. She's the one who wipes the chocolate off my lips and dries my tears when I cry.

No one knows what a kidnapper looks like. It's what I believed ever since I was a little girl. I was three when it happened. My mom always kept a close eye on me. When we went home, she let me put my pretty pink dress on and I became a princess. I wasn't scared of anything in my castle. My mom always said a dragon could take me away from her. We would always be safe if we were hand in hand if we left the castle. Nothing scared her more than the thought of me being kidnapped. I never knew I already was.

No one knows what a kidnapper looks like. She isn't anything like you think. She's pure and flawless. She doesn't smell like moldy tobacco as some girl's moms do. She smells of strawberry shampoo. There isn't alcohol in the house either. She has juice boxes. She doesn't leave her child waiting outside in the school yard for hours after school. She's early and waiting. She's *always* there.

***

It was particularly warm that Friday night, the night it happened. We already had the Christmas tree up and it sparkled into the darkness of my castle. It was supposed to snow, but the bright cloudless cranberry-apple orange skies showed the weathermen otherwise. It always snowed after Thanksgiving.

On that particular night, the dragon came to my castle, and took me away from my throne and the queen. It's what brought me to a small room with hard carpet and gray walls. They made me sit on an uncomfortable couch that matched the carpets in the claustrophobic room. The couch was picked because it matched, not because it gave any comfort to the person sitting in it. I felt like I was sitting in magazine article where the photos were selected from a gallery of stock photos.

I was ordered here by the court. They didn't know what to do with me. My mom would be going to jail. If I didn't understand it when I was a toddler, I did now: I wanted to get kidnapped. I had to go with my birth mother now. I would have to come back here every week. I was told I would have to live with my birth family again. I couldn't remember the bedroom where I spent my first few years and I didn't even remember if I had a brother or a sister or a cat or a dog. I only remember being an only child with my mom in a castle--a queen, and a princess.

A woman took me from the small stock photo room to a smaller room down a skinny hall. Dr. Frasier was my doctor and I was supposed to tell him my whole life.

"Hello, Gwen. I'm Henry," a tall, slender man with long arms covered with blue plaid sleeves came into the room.

"I thought your name was Dr. Frasier," I spoke quietly between my teeth. I heard him talk from behind the chair I was told to sit in. It made me uncomfortable. I didn't want to say hello back.

"You can call me that if want. Why don't we get started?"

I shrugged.

"I'm getting the feeling you don't want to be here. Am I right?" He asked. I shrugged again.

"Well, since we have the whole hour together, why don't we just get to know each other?" He pushed his round glasses back up his skinny nose.

"Why?"

"Because I want to get to know you."

"No. You don't," I said.

"Well, I can't force you talk so, what if I just talk?"

"Do whatever you want," I shoved my hands into the comfort of my pocket in the front of my sweatshirt.

"I understand this is difficult, Gwen."

"You don't know anything."

"You're right. Will you help me understand?"

"No," I said. He nodded again and scribbled something across the clipboard he held in his bony hand.

"Would you excuse me for a moment?" He asked. He left the room. I wanted my mommy and I knew how pathetic that sounded, especially when other girls my age wanted to get as far away from their mothers as possible.

I walked around the little room. He had a picture of his two boys on his desk. They looked so happy smiling at the camera in their swim trunks with Spider-Man and Capitan America on them and orange floaties on their arms.

I pushed the photo over and continued around the room. On the wall, hung diplomas from different schools. I wondered if any of them taught him what to do with cases like mine. Last week, my life was so normal. I went to school at seven forty-five and came home at three fifteen. Then my mom would feed me cookies or brownies with milk and she'd help me with my homework. I would go to gymnastics practice and we'd probably go out to dinner.

I heard Dr. Frasier talking to someone with a sweet voice in a different room that probably looked exactly like the one I was in. It wasn't the same lady's voice who brought me back here. I pushed another photo of the doctor's family over on his desk. I hated him and this time, I knew why. It wasn't him who was getting torn away from his family. It wasn't him who would never see his mom again.

He would get to go home at the end of the day. He would get to go home to his wife and his boys. He'd sit down to dinner at six and have ice cream at eight. He'd help his sons with their homework and tuck them into bed after bath time. Then, maybe he'd watch TV until 11 and join his wife upstairs. He would get to go home.

"Gwen?"

"What?"

"May I come in?" Dr. Frasier asked, like I had a say in the matter.

"It's your office," I said, going back to the couch.

"Oh my god, Gwen," the same strange woman's sweet voice followed Dr. Frasier's footsteps. She hugged me and I pushed her away. She smelled like rubbing alcohol and fake plastic flowers.

"Who are you? Who is this?" I asked.

"Gwen, this is Nora," Dr. Frasier said.

"I'm your mom," Nora said and rubbed her red nose with the back of her hand. Her eyes matched; they were puffy and runny.

"No, you're not," I said.

"Your birth mother," Dr. Frasier explained, like it even mattered.

"She's not my mom. *My* mom was ripped away from me last week," Her drugstore perfume was making me sick.

"I understand you're upset," Dr. Frasier said.

"Would you quit saying you 'understand' what I am because you don't!"

"We want to help," Dr. Frasier said.

I bit my tongue and held my breath. "Then take me home," I said. "Take me home to my mom. My *real* mom."

"Why don't we talk for a while then I can see what we can do about letting you see your mom."

"I can see her?" My voice lightened. Nora looked broken. I didn't care. She wasn't my mom and I didn't want her hugging me and I didn't want to talk to her.

"I'll see what I can do, but first, can we talk?"

"Fine," I sighed. The doctor gestured to Nora.

"I don't know what to say," she said. "What do I say?"

"Why don't we start simple?" The doctor suggested.

"Like what?" Nora asked, lost. I was gone for so, so long. She probably thought I was dead. I wondered how she was able to hang onto hope for 10 years. I wondered if she considered when it was time to let go.

"Well, where do you want to start, Gwen?"

I shrugged. I was beginning to think shrugging was now my only means of communication.

"Gwen, you have to participate a little," Dr. Frasier said.

I didn't want to, but I wanted to see my mom more.

"I don't know."

"It's okay," Nora said. "Do you have a favorite color?"

"Green."

"That's a lovely color," she said. My mom knew what my favorite color was. She wouldn't have to ask.

Dr. Frasier smiled at us, "why don't you tell us about some your hobbies."

"I would love to hear about them." Nora dried her eyes with a tissue.

"I like gymnastics," my voice flat. I only stayed in gymnastics because I happened to be talented and I would probably get a scholarship or something.

"That sounds fun," Nora said.

"I like it," I looked at Dr. Frasier, almost pleading for him to let me go.

"You did excellent today, Gwen. Thank you," he scribbled on his clipboard again. "Why don't you go out and wait for Hawkins to pick you up. I'll tell him we've agreed to let you see your mom." Hawkins was my own personal dragon left in charge of me. Apparently, I needed someone to report to and give me rides from place to place.

"Thanks," Nora and I both got up to leave.

"Nora?" he asked.

"Oh," she sat back down as I left the room.

When I did, I didn't close the door all the way. I knew they would be talking about me and I wanted to hear it. I slumped in my chair in the waiting room, putting my earbuds in. I didn't play music. As hard as I tried to listen, I couldn't hear them.

When Hawkins came in, he went back to the office where Nora and Dr. Frasier were. I suppose it should have concerned me they needed to talk, but I was just happy I would be seeing my *real* mom soon.

***

Inside the jail, a police officer took me to a room in the back. I ran in only to be stopped by a window. My mom sat in an iron chair with brown padding. She had tears in her eyes and stains on her cheeks. The cop led me to a similar chair and handed me a phone.

I sniffled, "Mommy?"

"Hey, there princess," she smiled, forcefully.

"I hate this. They made me meet Nora."

"Nora?"

"Yeah. They said she's my birth mother," I said. She stiffened with my explanation. Her cracked pink lips thinned and she grasped the phone tighter.

"I planned to tell you one day."

"Why didn't you tell me? I would have understood."

"No, you wouldn't have, Gwen."

"So? You're my mom. Not *Nora*. I don't care how you got me. You're my mom."

"Gwen," she smiled softly, "it doesn't justify what I've done. After all, I did take you from your family. I couldn't help it. I always knew I wanted to be a mother. I tried get pregnant and after several miscarriages, I gave up, though my desire to have a baby never changed. When I saw you in your mother's shopping cart. You had the cutest dress on. I remember it, it was blue overalls with patches and underneath you had a yellow shirt on. It had daisies on it."

"You remember that?" I asked.

"Of course. It was love at first sight. When I saw you, I knew you were the daughter I was meant to have. Then you smiled and reached for me, as young children do. You needed me too. So, I took you out of the cart when your mother turned away to grab a loaf of bread. I took you like it wasn't wrong. You were mine and it didn't matter. I held you on my hip and left the grocery store. When I got to my car, I realized I didn't have a car seat to put you in. Sure, I did have a car seat, but not one for a toddler."

"Why did you have a car seat?" I asked.

"I just had another miscarriage. I hadn't taken the car seat out yet. I couldn't. So, I drew the seatbelt across your chest in the back seat and tugged it tight. You talked to me on the way home, telling me everything like your favorite color and how old you were. That night I realized what I had done, but I had no regret. I loved you. There were times when I would think of your mother. I couldn't believe what I had done to her. I understood how she was suffering. I knew I had to make things right and I needed to take you back to her, but I couldn't. I loved you too much and you were mine," she said and couldn't look me in the eyes. I didn't care, though, she was still my mom. I understood why she didn't tell me, though. How do you tell your daughter you're not hers? How do you explain to your child you kidnapped her? It was all too much.

***

I cried as a cop took me out to the office of the jail where Hawkins stood.

"Ready to go, Gwen?" He asked. I glared at him. He put his hand on my shoulder and I shrugged it off. I wished people would stop trying to comfort me because there was only one person who could comfort me and she was locked away like a criminal and she was the nicest, most loving person in the world.

After meeting with Dr. Frasier, I was promised I'd get to go home and get some of my things. Hawkins didn't want me to take too long in my room, but I would take the longest time possible. I wanted to stay there forever.

I started in my closet. I reached up to the top shelf in my closet and grabbed a pair of black canvas tennis shoes. When I grabbed them, another shoebox fell down and hit me in the head.

"Damnit," I sighed and I started crying. I slid down the wall of my closet to the plush carpet and held my knees as I cried and picked up the box.

Some photos had showered around me when the box fell. I picked them up and smiled at my little three-year-old self in a pink dress. I put it back in the box and picked up the next photo. They were all of me at that age. I didn't find any of me being any younger than three. I shoved the photos back in the box and threw it on the shelf, biting my lower lip. How had I never noticed I've never seen a baby picture of myself? Why hadn't I ever *asked* to see a baby picture? How could I have been so blind that there was something off?

I shoved my clothes in my duffel bag and grabbed my little stuffed frog off my bed and the pictures of my mom that I had pinned to the wall. They were the ones from a photo booth in the mall. The five pictures of us were silly. We had sunglasses that were bigger than our faces and horribly ugly hats on. I wished to go back to when we spent the whole day shopping at all my favorite stores. We shared a soft pretzel and I had a cherry Slurpee, she had the blue raspberry. We only filled our cups half full so we had room to mix our flavors, like we always did. I guess I never noticed how my mom wasn't so much a mom, my best friend.

***

That night, I slept in what had become my home for the past week. I had a bedroom I shared with three other girls. I didn't want to leave the half-way house. At least here, I wasn't the only one with problems. I didn't have parents who hated me and shoved me aside. I didn't have parents who died and left me behind. I didn't have parents who were drug addicts. I actually had *two* moms. I had two moms who *loved* me and *wanted* me.

After I ate breakfast, Hawkins drove me to the house that was apparently the home where I spent my first few years.

"Would you like to see your room?" Nora asked when Hawkins finally left.

"Um, sure," I nodded. She led me to a little room in the back of the house. Behind the white door, the pink walls suffocated me. There was only one small window, covered by pink and white plaid print curtains.

"It's nice," I lied, but I was trying. Nora was hurting as bad as I was and I wasn't making anything any easier by sulking around and throwing tantrums.

"We can paint it," she said, "maybe green."

"Can I confess something?" I asked, throwing my bag on the pink covered twin bed.

"Sure," she sat down by my bag.

"I lied. My favorite color isn't green. It's purple."

"Dark purple?"

"How did you know?"

"It's my favorite color too," she smiled.

"I'm sorry I lied."

"I understand," she said. I blinked.

"You do?"

"I know you're scared. Who wouldn't be?"

"Wow. You do understand," I thought.

"Why don't I go get you a snack?"

"Um, okay."

When she left, I only took one shirt out and hung it on the rod in the closet. Now it shared space with little dresses that hung on little plastic hangers. I wanted to pretend they were from a new baby, but I knew they weren't. She never wanted to accept I was gone. She always thought I would come back home.

I went to the living room with one of the dresses. Nora was just setting down a plate with cut up apple slices on the coffee table.

"I'm really sorry," I said.

"It's okay, Gwen. I understand why you lied," she said.

"No, not about that. I meant, about this." I held up the dress.

"Oh. So you put your clothes away?"

"Yes and no," I said, "I was hanging a shirt up and I saw this."

"And that's why you're sorry?"

"I'm sorry because I got taken," I said "I didn't think about how you are feeling. I'm sorry for acting like such a brat to you yesterday," I tossed the dress on a slouching arm chair. She smiled at me and sat down on the couch.

"Can I show you something?" She brushed the cushion next to hers. I sat down by her, slowly. I never said it would be easy to accept what was happening to me. I just said I'd try.

"Sure." I said and took an apple slice from the plate, dipping it in the peanut butter. She jerked the drawer in the coffee table open and took a black photo album. She pointed at the first picture. I could tell it was her, but she was much younger and her hair was much darker. Her skin was pink and dewy and a baby was in her arms.

"Is this me?" I asked, scooting closer to her. She nodded and pointed to the next picture. The same baby was in a car seat. A man sat by her. He had lines around his young bright brown eyes. I guessed he was where I got my eyes-not my mom's.

"Who's that?" I asked anyway.

"Your father," She said.

"Really? Is he here?"

"No," She shook her head.

"Is he at work or something?" I took a bite of the apple I had in my hand.

"Probably."

"What do you mean. Oh," I said.

"We divorced six months after…"

"I'm so sorry." I said and looked at the picture again.

"It's not your fault." She said.

"It kind of is my fault though."

"No it's not, it's-."

"Please don't say it's my mom's fault." I begged.

"I just wish I knew why she did it," she said.

"She wanted a baby," I said, still looking at the photo. Nora didn't say anything and flipped the page in the photo album. She started explaining different pictures and telling me stories of how cute and how smart I was as a baby.

She took me to dinner after. I told her how it was tradition between me and my mother to go out to dinner every Monday and Friday night after gymnastics practice.

"Gwen," she said with a cheek full of ice cream we ordered for desert.

"Yes?"

"Thank you for telling me everything."

"Thanks for listening." I said.

"I don't want to take you away from your mom," she said. I looked at the lump of strawberry ice cream on the red plate on the center of the table. "I mean; I want to get to know her too."

I smiled, "I think you would like her."

"I bet I would."

***

Months later, when the court date rolled around, things had started to settle down. I got used to my new life. I made new friends and I met my whole family. Even my dad. They all still missed me so much and I was doing my best to not freak out or get angry. I still freaked out though and at times, I was still angry, but I was healing.

The morning of the court date, I dressed in my best clothes and rehearsed what I was going to say to the judge. I had never been so nervous in my life. Other kids my age were nervous to give a speech or a presentation in class, but I was nervous I would never get to see my mom again even though Nora had promised she wouldn't let it happen. She was going to show the court my mother wasn't the villain in my story. I took one last look at myself in the mirror. I was taken aback by how different I looked than my mom and how much I looked like Nora.

After court, the sentencing had been made; second degree kidnapping. My mom would be in prison for five years and for those five years, I wouldn't get to see her because I was still a minor and she was now a threat to my well-being. I hated the judge. I hated the jury. I hated myself. I hated I couldn't prove the jury wrong. I hated they didn't see my mom as a grieving mother reaching for her own piece of happiness.

I walked out of the courthouse hugging myself with Hawkins behind me. Nora was at my side. I took her hand. A mess of people filled the streets. There were men with cameras and women with microphones. They were all shouting different things at me. As I walked to Hawkins car, a lady shoved a microphone in my face.

"Did you ever know you were kidnapped?" She asked me. I remembered what Hawkins and our lawyers said; I didn't have to reply to any of the press. In fact, it would be best if I just stayed quiet and kept my mouth shut. But, I couldn't.

"No one knows what being kidnapped feels like." I said, looking up at Nora. I smiled softly at her, then back at the lady, "but, *I* do."

Jamie Wright is a full-time student at Colorado State University double majoring in English, concertation in creative writing and History. Born in Wyoming, she learned how to drive a tractor before a car. Now, Jamie lives in Fort Collins, Colorado with her two fur babies: cats Salem Anne and Kaysee Lou. In 2017, she won first place in the fiction competition at the Colorado State University Celebrating Undergraduate Research and Creativity competition. Deep Purple is her second published piece. You can follow Jamie on Tumblr at jwrightswrites and her website http://jamiesmail.wixsite.com/thoughtsoftheheart

Living Springs Publishers

Living Springs Publishers LLP is a family owned, independent publishing company based in Centennial, Colorado. We chose the name Living Springs Publishers to honor our roots in the Living Springs area of Eastern Colorado. When we first started Living Springs Publishers we had two very specific goals in mind: To finish and publish Henry's book "What is a Hero" and Dan's novel "The Toastmaster". These goals were quickly met. Henry and Dan are both working on new books that will be available soon.

We then decided to give other writers an opportunity to have their work made available to the public. The idea for our "Stories Through the Ages" book series was born in a brainstorming session among several of our family members, both old and young. Entries began pouring in for the College Edition and for the Baby Boomer Plus contests and we were on our way. We are extremely proud of our first three books and the authors who submitted their stories. We plan on these contests continuing for many more years.

In 2018 we started a new endeavor called Legacy Books. We want to help people create a legacy of their family history in words and pictures. Something permanent for those family members who follow and something fluid that can be updated with the passage of time.   Visit us at www.livingspringspublishers.com.

About our Contests

Living Springs Publishers "Stories Through The Ages" short story contests features stories written by people in different segments of the population. There is no prompt for the contests, stories may be about any topic. For each contest the story from the finalists is included in our "Stories Through The Ages" collection. Each edition of the book is published annually. In addition first, second and third place finalists receive cash prizes.

The Baby Boomers Plus edition is open to anyone who was born 1964 or earlier. The word count for this contest is 700 – 4000 words.

The College Edition is open to any person enrolled at a Nationally Accredited United States college or university at the time of submission. The word count for this contest is 1500 – 4000 words.

The Generations XYZ edition is for anyone who was born 1965 – 1996. Please let us know if you are interested in this contest. If we get enough interest we will open submissions.

www.livingspringspublishers.com/index.php/contests/